BRUTE FORCE

BETRAYALS

Also by Dean Wesley Smith and Kristine Kathryn Rusch
Published by Del Rey Books:

THE TENTH PLANET
THE TENTH PLANET: OBLIVION
THE TENTH PLANET: FINAL ASSAULT
X-MEN

BRUTE FORCE
BETRAYALS

Dean Wesley Smith

BALLANTINE BOOKS • NEW YORK

A Del Rey® Book
Published by The Ballantine Publishing Group
Copyright © 2002 by Microsoft Corporation

All rights reserved under International and Pan-American Copyright Conventions. Published in the United States by The Ballantine Publishing Group, a division of Random House, Inc., New York, and simultaneously in Canada by Random House of Canada Limited, Toronto.

Xbox, the Xbox Logos, Brute Force, and Digital Anvil are registered trademarks or trademarks of Microsoft Corporation in the United States and/or other countries and are used under license from owner.

Del Rey is a registered trademark and the Del Rey colophon is a registered trademark of Random House, Inc.

www.delreydigital.com

ISBN 0-345-45850-8

Manufactured in the United States of America

First Edition: October 2002

OPM   10   9   8   7   6   5   4   3

For Bill Trojan,
thanks for everything

Acknowledgments

For performance above and beyond the call of duty, special thanks to Digital Anvil's Erin Roberts and Tim Fields, and Microsoft's Franchise Development Group, especially editor Doug Zartman.

Acknowledgments

Chapter One

Let's face it—if a controller wants one of us dead, we're dead. Accidents happen—well, sometimes they happen on purpose.

—Legman,
from a speech given during the
Operatives' Rebellion, intercepted by Intel

"Is that bonded armor?"

The voice barely registered over the noise the shuttle was making as it hit the upper atmosphere. If Tex hadn't known better, he would have sworn the entire ship was going to shake apart.

He had used these ten-seater corporate shuttles before. They were fast, they could land just about anywhere either on a runway or in vertical mode, and no military bothered with them, since they usually carried the rich and powerful. They were perfect for getting on and off planet without attracting attention.

This particular shuttle sported leather seats, a bathroom that Tex had no trouble fitting into—even with his stature—and carpet that was far too thick. He had tripped twice getting on board with his gear.

And just about now the shuttle was bouncing hard as it headed down toward the surface of Dower. At first glance it didn't seem the sort of planet a corporate jet might be heading to visit. Dower was covered with more rock and sand than should be allowed in one location. It had no real plant or animal life, but it boasted a human base, half of which was hidden beneath the surface. When Tex and his team finished with that base, it would vanish into the next sandstorm.

The planet had no official name. It was nothing but a number on the star charts; that's how valueless it was. But Seton, their controller, had taken to calling it after the name of their target, the Dowers, and it had stuck for Tex.

Dower itself wasn't actually a name; it was an acronym for the five men who founded this particular group of troublemakers.

Only the pilot and the three operatives were on board the flight. No operative ever paid a pilot much attention, even though they were a very critical part of almost every mission. They weren't going to be involved with the fighting, so operatives simply tended to call them "pilot" and leave it at that. They didn't even bother to learn their code names.

Tex had made his way to the back of the cabin, and sat facing away from the main cockpit, taking up the entire last group of four facing seats with his large body and his equipment. Conversations had been minimal during the six-hour flight from their launch point in the Decker star system, and he had spent most of that time checking and double-checking, making sure everything about his weapons and armor was ready to go.

"That bonded armor?" The question came again.

Tex glanced up over his shoulder at Rees, the scout on this mission, who stood with one hand on the back of a seat, riding out the bumps like this was a slow boat on a calm ocean. He stepped closer when Tex looked at him, so Rees stood more in Tex's line of sight.

Compared with Tex's massive frame, Rees was no more than a stick that looked as if it could be easily broken. But Tex knew Rees was much stronger and more dangerous than his short blond hair, deep blue eyes, and long bony fingers would lead someone to believe. On their last mission, Tex had seen Rees poke one of his armored fingers right through the heart of a small-time crook who had given him some back talk. He was one of the best scouts Tex had ever worked with. And the most cold-blooded.

Tex respected him, and Rees knew it.

"Yeah, bonded," Tex said, patting the armor on the seat beside him. "And reflective."

"Yeah, mine, too," Rees said. "Spent more than I should for it, though."

Tex only nodded at that. Bonded armor was

basically standard plate, with a molecularly bonded coat of plastic that made the armor a good 10 percent stronger. Tex figured that the extra 10 percent might just be worth the money, considering how close he had come to being killed on the last few missions. He couldn't spend the money if he were dead, so why not use a little of it to keep himself alive?

Reflective coating on the armor was pretty much a necessity anytime they were going up against human targets, as they were today. Humans liked lasers.

"You worried about the Dowers?" Rees asked, bracing himself as the shuttle hit a hard bump. Tex held his hand on his armor to keep it on the seat beside him. Even Rees, a man who seemed to have perfect balance, had to move his foot sideways a few inches to remain standing.

Tex laughed. "Always worried about any mission. Better to expect the worst and come out thinkin' it was easy."

That motto had gotten him through a good fifty missions so far. Tex didn't figure to change it now. More than once, by expecting and preparing for the worst, he had saved his own life.

Actually the twisted feeling in his gut was worse this time than on any previous mission Tex could remember. Usually by this point he had grown accustomed to that low-level nagging fear that came with going into a fight. He used the fear to push himself. No mission was ever fear free, but this one bothered him more than he wanted to admit, especially to another operative.

"Yeah," Rees said. "Good way of lookin' at it. But I've still got an extra bad feeling about this target. I heard talk that we're not the first ops the Dowers have dealt with."

"So they got lucky," Tex said, shrugging as he took part of his leg armor and started to strap it on, making sure it left his ankles plenty of freedom of movement, yet protected what it was supposed to protect. He had heard the same rumor, about a lost ops team, as well. But he had figured it was just another controller yanking Seton's chain.

Commander Seton was their controller, at least on this mission, and he had fought a pretty nasty fight to get the three of them assigned to it. So nasty rumors about the Dowers would have come with the territory. It seemed to Tex that lately the infighting between the controllers was getting worse, though, and ops like him always tended to pay the price.

Besides, Tex couldn't figure out what the Dowers could have done to repel any decent ops team. From all the intelligence reports Tex had reviewed, the group Rees was worried about was a gang of rogue asteroid miners, based on this barren planet, who had found more lucrative uses for their piloting, navigation, and boarding skills.

They raided cargo ships flying past this system, usually leaving the crew members dead, or wishing they were dead. The Dowers had made a name for themselves with their brutality, but their kind wasn't unusual in deserted systems like this one.

The regional military of the neighboring system had made some attempts to stop the Dowers, without success, and the result had been high losses in ships and lives. It seemed this Dowers group had some nasty firepower in its ships, but there was no report about anyone taking them on the ground. And that was exactly how Tex and his team were going to finish them.

And with any luck, they would bring back some pretty valuable bounty. The Dowers had managed over the last year to raid some rich cargo ships, including a Seer ship just a few months before. Seton wanted those cargoes back, or the money from the cargoes, and Tex wouldn't mind getting that for him. After Tex and the other ops got their share, of course.

In this business, there was always a price.

Tex finished the last inspection of his armor and glanced up. Rees still just stood there, hand on the back of the seat, riding the bumping shuttle floor like he had been born with the ground moving. The worry was etched into his pale skin and blue eyes. Tex had been on five different missions with Rees over the years. Not once had Tex seen Rees this worried.

And Rees' worry didn't help Tex's own. He had to get Rees past this and get them both focused on the job at hand. A little tension was fine, but too much cut into focus and could cost an op his life.

"You just tell me where the Dowers are at," Tex said. He patted one of his two favorite weapons, an eight-barrel Branson machine gun called a *minigun* by some joker long ago who more than likely couldn't even pick one up, let alone fire it and remain standing. "Me and Branson here will do the rest, knock down their buildings, and we'll all go home rich."

Unlike most operatives, Tex could aim and fire a Branson minigun with one hand, and he was able to fire two at once. Actually he *liked* to fire two at once, if the situation demanded. On the last mission with Rees he'd knocked down an entire three-story building by rushing in with both Bransons blasting. Luckily the building had fallen in the other direction and had buried their targets in the rubble. Rees kidded him about it for a week.

Rees smiled, but the smile didn't reach his cold eyes. "Just make sure the walls fall away from us again."

"Deal," Tex said.

Rees nodded. "Good to have you along on this one."

"Good to be along," Tex said.

With that Rees turned and headed back up the

aisle to his seat. They would be touching down in ten minutes, and if the pilot and the radar jammer hadn't done the trick, he and the team might land in the "soup" right out the door.

Tex glanced over his shoulder at Toole, the sniper for this mission, who had been sitting in the front seat the entire flight. Toole had somehow managed to afford some Szorilium armor made up of an alien plastic that had unique properties for absorbing and distributing damage to a much greater degree than the standard armor. The stuff was very expensive and hard to come by. How Toole had managed it was anyone's guess. She did things like that and never told anyone how.

She stood no more than five feet tall and could fire off a shot faster than any human being Tex had ever seen. Tex had been on two missions with her and still marveled at how good she was with her sniper rifle. She also carried a Black Pistol, knives, and a pretty good load of shrapnel and gas grenades, a larger number than he had seen a sniper carry before.

If Toole ever got afraid, she never mentioned it to Tex or ever showed it in the slightest. She was about as calm, collected, and coldhearted as they came.

"Five minutes," came the voice over the loudspeaker.

The pilot's warning turned Tex back around in

his seat. The flight had smoothed a little since they settled into a glide path through the atmosphere. He snapped the last of his armor into place, double-checked his minigun ammunition clips, then stood in the aisle, and secured them in his belt and pockets.

Then he slung the two miniguns over his shoulders, hooked the straps, and made sure both were easy to pull down and into position. Under the weight of those guns he actually felt better. So far, not much had gotten in his way when he went at them with both guns firing.

Finally, Tex strapped on a belt loaded with grenades. He had three shrapnel, three gas, and two incendiary—two more grenades than normal for an ops agent. But he was big enough and could carry them.

He hoped he didn't have to use the incendiary until they had the shuttle loaded with bounty and were ready to leave. Incendiary grenades did too much damage of the type that cost them goods. But they were nasty in a hard fight, and great for finishing off a target building so it could never be used again.

He did one more quick double check, then turned, and headed up the short aisle toward where Rees and Toole were standing.

As the scout, Rees would be first out the door, and he would go left. Toole would follow and go right, scanning for a good sniper position. Tex would come out, guns ready, and head right up the middle.

"Grab on to something," the pilot said. "Coming in hard and fast."

Tex spread his feet, braced his hip against the leather seat, and pressed one hand against the roof of the shuttle, giving himself four anchor points. He'd ridden in through many rough landings in that position and never once been jarred loose.

The pilot had been right. As Tex watched on the forward monitor, the shuttle swept in over an orange-and-black rock ledge and then dropped almost straight down to the bottom of a rock canyon floor, hitting hard. It seemed to bounce; then it yanked to a sudden stop.

With a loud clang, the hatch of the shuttle dropped outward, letting in the bright, almost white light of the planet's surface.

Before the hatch could even touch the ground, Rees was out, rifle ready, disappearing into the swirling cloud of sand and dust that the shuttle had kicked up with its landing. They often counted on that cloud to give them a few seconds' cover that could send fatal bullets astray and get the enemy to stick their necks out.

Toole was not more than a step behind Rees, also vanishing into the sand and dust.

Tex took two seconds to get down the rest of the aisle and into the white light and hot air of the planet's surface. He had a minigun pulled and in position as he stepped forward and went down the short ramp.

By the time he reached the bottom, the swirling sand from the shuttle's landing had begun to settle, revealing the stark brown-and-red landscape around him. His weight sank him a half inch into the brown-and-gold sand with each step forward as he scouted the area for cover and any sign of the enemy.

The shuttle pilot had brought them down between two rock mounds, in a rock-faced canyon, from the looks of it not more than a half a klick from the Dower base. The rocks were sandstone, with swirling red-and-gold-and-brown markings. The sky overhead was a faint blue, with no clouds and light that seemed almost white. Everything looked stark and very hot.

Rees was scrambling up the mound of boulders on the left, moving like a monkey going up a tree.

Toole had moved over to the boulders on the right, taken up a cover position, and had her rifle and scope trained down the sand-filled valley toward their target, looking for anything that might be moving.

Behind Tex the shuttle door slammed shut, and in a blast of more windblown sand, the pilot lifted off and sped down the rock-walled valley away from the target and their position, staying as low as he could for as long as he could. Tex knew he would land again in some hidden valley to wait for their retrieval call.

The silence of the alien planet slammed over Tex as the shuttle vanished, increasing the sensation of the heat and the thin air. He stood, his machine gun aimed down the valley in front of him.

Nothing moved.

The seconds ticked on, but he had no intention of changing his position until the scout gave the clear signal.

Around him the heat seemed to shimmer in waves off the brown-and-golden sand. He had been in a lot of hellholes over the years of being an operative. This one looked like it might rank among the hottest. No wonder nothing grew here. It couldn't.

"Clear," Rees said, his voice loud in Tex's communication link in his helmet. "Toole, hill to your left gives a good firing point if you can climb it."

"I can climb it," Toole said, turning and starting up the rock slope.

"Tex, we wait for a sixty count to give her time."

Tex stood, the sweat starting to drip off his forehead. "Copy that."

Ahead, the sand valley looked like a simple road. He wanted to move now, to stride down that sand valley with guns blazing, walk right into the Dowers, cutting them apart like so many clay targets.

He could feel the excitement starting to mount in his gut. This was the reason he had joined operations. He loved the action. It had gotten him excited, from the first time he'd taken the oath after boot camp.

"Thirty count," Rees said.

"Almost in position," Toole said.

Thirty seconds.

It seemed too long. Tex could feel his blood racing, taste the salt of his sweat as it ran down his face. There was nothing better than a good fight for the right cause. And defending the interests of the Confederation, protecting cargo vessels, and making a little money along the way were all about as good as he could think of.

"Let's move," Rees said, coming up from behind a rock near the top of the hill and heading forward.

Tex strode out, his feet sinking into the sand with each step, his two machine guns held out, pointed forward, ready.

It was time to fight. He loved that more than anything.

Deputy Director Petrie sat, his back to the door of his plush office and facing away from his large, real wood desk, pretending to read a report outlining the situation on a planet called Cent Three. It was one of those reports he wasted very little time on and cared about even less. What he really was doing was waiting. Alternately reading and staring out over the fantastic view of the cliffside city of Wren, he simply waited, letting the comforting movement of his personal-fitted chair ease his back.

His office had to be one of the best furnished ones in the sector. It had everything, including a fully stocked bar, a luxurious bath, shower, and hot tub in an adjoining room, and the best leather furniture imported from Winston. The wood desk alone had cost him more than a dozen miners made in a year. It had been handmade in Winston from birch and oak trees taken there by the first settlers from Earth.

Wren, a city of almost a half million, covered the cliff face below his office tower, the valley floor, and the facing cliff across the valley. The charm of Wren was in its hanging gardens and year-round blooming flowers of just about every color. The city had been called one of the most beautiful places in the Known Worlds, and that statement would get no argument from Petrie. He was just glad this was where his boss had decided to establish the headquarters for this branch of the Protectorate.

He would keep it here when he took over.

Damian Petrie was an immensely powerful man, and he knew it. But very few others did. He liked it that way. It gave him more freedom to do what he needed to do, when he needed to do it.

There were nine administrative regions of the Protectorate, each covering about six systems. Petrie was the Deputy Director of Region Six, which included the Anaeas system and the Ulysses system, among others.

His boss, Director Edwards, had long since lost his edge. If all went well, with only a few more missions, Petrie would soon push Edwards aside and take a seat on the Protectorate board.

The Protectorate was the policing arm of the Confederation. His duty as regional director would be, on the most basic level, to enforce the Confed laws applicable to the worlds in his jurisdiction. He was responsible for keeping the peace between them. To do this, he kept tabs on dissident groups through information provided by Intel. He deployed navy gunboats or cruisers on "training exercises" when a show of strength was needed, and when actual force was required, he didn't hesitate to dispatch teams of highly trained operatives.

And when ops were involved, that opened up a whole new set of opportunities. It never hurt if he made a little extra money and did a few favors for the right people in the right places. In the pursuit of power, wealth and friends came in handy, especially for a man in his position.

Of course, such favors and certain operations had made him one of the richest men on Wren. And had made him a few serious enemies in the process. These enemies didn't worry him much, though. He loved making extra money, but what he wanted more than anything else was to take down Deputy Edwards and move into his office.

The door from his secretary's area slid open with a faint whoosh. He couldn't hear her steps on the thick, blue carpet, but he could sense her behind him.

Cannie was a short, slim woman with close-chopped bright red hair, and she was completely loyal to him. He had directed the rescue of her oldest son from a group of malcontents on Thera Six shortly after he had hired her. She had been at his side completely and without question ever since that day.

"Sir."

"Yes?" He pretended to keep reading the worthless report.

"A message, sir," Cannie said, "that makes no sense."

"From whom, and what does it say?" he asked, keeping his voice level. He turned to look into her eyes. He hoped this was the message he had been waiting for.

"It says, 'Arranged.' " She shook her head, clearly puzzled. "The name on the message was only the letter *D*."

"Arranged?" He pretended to look puzzled, even though he knew exactly what the message meant and exactly who it was from.

"Strange," he said, shaking his head. "More than likely meant for some other department. Give it to me. I'll ask around."

She nodded, seemingly relieved that something wasn't going on that she didn't know about. Cannie would be surprised by just how much happened without her knowledge. This short but to-the-point message had come from a contact with one of the groups he was supposed to be suppressing. A very large payment had been made to one of his special accounts. A hidden and private account.

In exchange for this large payment, a number of things would and would not happen. Ships from the Confed Navy would not be in a certain area of space at a certain time, so that the alien religious group called the Sword of Shadoon would have the opportunity to explore some ruins unobserved. And an underground city on a planet in the same system would be . . . disrupted.

Petrie didn't care, actually, why the Shadoon wanted to explore those alien ruins. The fact that the Shadoon wanted to explore a dead, non-Confed world had no real impact, as far as he could tell, on the overall security of the Confed. The aliens' inexplicable beliefs had just earned him a nice chunk of security for a rainy day. Nothing lost and a lot gained.

He smiled and turned to stare back out over the fantastic view of the city, admiring the cliffs and valley floor below him. Sometimes he loved being near the top. It afforded him so much freedom.

And being *on* top would be just that much better.

Hawk moved silently along the wall, her back almost rubbing the rough brick so that she could keep an eye on the street, both ahead and behind. Above her, on both sides, the black windows of silent buildings towered three and four stories in the air, making the street into a narrow canyon. The air around her was heavy and damp, the near-dawn city almost completely silent. The only sound was a ship's horn from the nearby harbor.

Here in the subtropical lowlands of the planet Jasper's largest continent, everything smelled of oranges, sweet and ripe. Now, with the air thick and still, the smell was cloying and made breathing feel a lot like trying to swallow syrup.

Hawk had hated the feeling of the air, hated the stench, from the moment they had stepped off the transport that had brought her and the rest of the team here. It would take a lot of long, hot showers before she would get this place off her skin.

The city around her, the capital of Jasper, was named Blossom, more than likely for the smell. Anyone who ever came here left calling it Stink. She had heard that a hundred times, but until now she had never really understood it. It seemed that even people who loved oranges hated the smell after a few days.

No surprise to her. She'd been here only an hour and wanted the smell gone. She had never been a fan of oranges anyway, but after this, she doubted she would ever be able to eat one again.

Her stomach twisted, and she forced herself to take a deep breath. This mission had bothered her right from the moment it had been assigned, but lately every mission seemed to do that. More experienced ops told her that fear never really went away. The key to surviving was to accept it and move on.

Another deep breath of the thick air and she pushed the worry away, focused on the task at hand. Serving as point in this stealth-heavy op, she was responsible for assessing the tactical situation and directing the fire of her teammates, at least until their cover was blown and the real slugging began.

A block down the street was their target's headquarters, a three-story warehouse with no markings and no windows. That warehouse was the headquarters of the National Renovation

Movement. The NRM was a violent dissident group bent on the overthrow of this planet's government, the government that was a member of the Confederation, with a seated delegate in the Quorum.

From what intelligence had said, someone in the Protectorate had been tipped off that the NRM was going to stage an attack on the Confederation embassy here in Blossom.

Her team's job was to stop it. Objective one.

Objective two was to take out, or at least slow down, the NRM in the process.

Of course, if everything went exactly right, they would end up with the NRM treasury that their controller had told them resided in a vault somewhere in that warehouse. She had every intention of making sure a large chunk of that treasury ended up in her bank account when this mission was over.

She pressed her back against the rough brick just inside a doorway and stared ahead. There were two guards posted on the roof, and two more in windows across the street. She couldn't see others, but more than likely there were more guards on the far side of the building, watching that street, as well.

Their intel was that the old warehouse, besides housing the vault, had been turned into living quarters for upward of one hundred National Renovation Movement soldiers. The place had kitchens, bunk rooms, game rooms, and training rooms, as well as a large arsenal.

That supply of weapons and explosives would be the NRM's downfall, if her team had anything to say about it.

She touched her communications link. "Flint? You in position?"

"Affirmative," Flint said, her voice coming through clearly in Hawk's ear piece.

Flint was the second member of the team, and the one Hawk trusted most. She was the last of the generation of "synthetics," cyborg warriors created for the Machine Wars. Her augmented abilities gave Flint inhuman reflexes and precision, making her the deadliest sniper Hawk had ever seen, or could even imagine. They had been on only two missions together, but already Hawk wouldn't choose anyone else as her sniper, covering her every move.

Right now Flint had stationed herself on the corner of a four-story building that overlooked not only the street Hawk was on, but the roof and main door of their target, as well. Flint wasn't more than a hundred paces from either, and at that range, she could shoot a fly off someone's bare skin and not even leave a mark.

"Brit?" Hawk asked, "how about you and Rule?"

"In position," Brit's husky voice answered. "Just give the word."

Brit and Rule were the other two operatives on the team. Together they had come to Operations from the Navy, and since then they had been teamed often. They both loved any kind of heavy weapon. Both wore miniguns strapped on their backs and enough grenades to bring down a city block. On this mission Brit also carried a particle beam cannon and Rule had a Thermalite missile launcher. The plan was that after Hawk and Flint took out the guards, Brit and Rule would move up into position.

Brit would then use the cannon to open a hole in the side of the building where the target's armory was located, and Rule would blow it all up with a Thermalite missile, using the target's own explosives to destroy as much as possible.

That was the plan, but Hawk knew that plans rarely went exactly as they were supposed to.

Also, given the speed with which the capital's local police and fire departments tended to respond, this mission, from first shot to evacuation on the orbital shuttle, could not take longer than fifteen minutes. And that included searching for the vault and loading the treasury, if they found it.

From what Hawk had been told, the attack on the Confed embassy was scheduled for eight this morning, local time. It was five now. With luck, they'd catch most of the target members inside the building when they hit it.

"Okay, Flint," Hawk said, glancing at her watch. "Start taking them out."

"Copy that."

A moment later the muffled sound of a shot, almost like someone dropping a fruit on the sidewalk, cut the thick smell in the air. The guard Hawk could see on the top of the building slumped forward, but luckily he didn't drop his weapon over the edge.

A second shot by Flint took out the entire side of another guard's head. That guy made a little more noise dying.

Hawk flicked on her stealth field and moved quickly down the sidewalk to get into a position to take out the two guards in the facing windows, the ones Flint couldn't see. In stealth mode, she couldn't be seen or heard, but the field consumed a lot of energy, so she used it only sparingly.

Around her, while she was in stealth, everything had a watery look to it, as if she were staring through a fish tank. In training she had gotten used to the stealth distortion, and now it didn't bother her. Stealth mode redirected light around her, which meant someone looking directly at her while she passed might see a strange deformity moving through the air, like a heat wave coming off hot desert sand.

She reached cover and dropped out of stealth mode. She swung around and took aim at the guard in the window. He was talking on some sort of communication device, and clearly he was not happy. He must have seen one of the other guards go down.

Hawk aimed at a spot right between his eyes and silenced him.

The sound of her rifle seemed loud to her ears, but nowhere near as loud as the breaking glass as her bullet went through the window, shattering it before hitting her target.

She swung upward, zeroed in on the next target one story above the first, and killed him, as well. This time, because of the different angle, the glass in the window didn't break.

"Flint," Hawk ordered, "stay in position and take out whatever comes out that front door or appears on that roof."

"Copy," Flint said.

"Brit and Rule," she said, "time to light 'em up, cause a few morning fireworks."

"On our way," Brit said.

Hawk knew it would take them a good fifteen seconds to move up, get into position, and fire. Fifteen long seconds that might mean the difference between success or failure with this target. What she had to do was get back out of the way and help Flint guard Brit and Rule while they fired their big weapons.

Another faint thump echoed through the canyon between the buildings. That indicated Flint had fired again.

Hawk went back into stealth mode and sprinted for a position in a doorway across from their target and out of the blast range.

Flint fired twice more, quickly, but Hawk couldn't see her targets.

Hawk had no doubt that this was going to get interesting very quickly.

A few seconds later, Brit and Rule thudded into sight around a corner, making no attempt to move silently along the paved street. Their boot steps echoed up the canyon of buildings. As they appeared, an NRM guard poked his head out a door across the street from them. That building wasn't on any of the intelligence reports Hawk had read. Not a good sign.

The guy started to raise his rifle, and Hawk killed him instantly.

"Nice shooting," Brit said. Then he stopped, yanked up his particle beam cannon, and aimed it at the corner of the warehouse building, just about where the second floor would be.

The cannon fire echoed through the street like a thunderbolt, rattling windows and doors and breaking out the front glass of a store ten paces away from Hawk.

The cannon did its job. The side of the warehouse just seemed to explode inward, sending a huge cloud of dust and smoke billowing upward.

Hawk could see that the explosion had taken

out a number of men who had clearly been scrambling for weapons inside the NRM armory.

Rule fired his Thermalite missile launcher. The sound couldn't be heard over the explosions in the warehouse, but the rocket he fired streaked straight toward the new opening in the corner of the warehouse, as if it were being pulled on a string.

The next explosion shook the ground under Hawk and knocked some bricks off the wall around her.

"It's good!" Rule shouted.

Explosion after explosion rocked the warehouse as the target's own weapons and supplies were set off, working to destroy their own headquarters.

Hawk snapped down her dust goggles and kept a sharp eye out around them as the corner of the warehouse seemed to just vanish in clouds of rolling fire and smoke.

Then it looked like someone had kicked an anthill. Pouring out the side and front doors of the warehouse, swarms of well-armed NRM members hit the streets, ducking flying shrapnel as the corner of the building they were leaving exploded and collapsed.

Both Brit and Rule tossed aside their cannons and grabbed their machine guns, smiles on their faces. They loved a good fight.

From what Hawk could tell, given all the

targets pouring out of that smoking warehouse alive, she and Flint and Brit and Rule were in for just that.

Chapter Two

An Operations Division agent can expect no medals. His reward is living. And if he is good, he lives well.

—Wallis DeClark,
Protectorate Board member
overseeing the Operations Division

Tex did his best to ignore the heat and the sweat dripping down his face as he moved steadily, step-by-step in the soft sand, up the red-rocked valley toward the Dower encampment. From what he had heard of the gunshots, Toole had already killed two forward guards from her position on the rock cliff overlooking the base. And Rees had told them he had taken out another guard by sneaking up on him and opening his throat.

Tex kept his machine gun aimed ahead as he walked. It was set on rapid fire and was filled with armor-piercing rounds that could cut through just about anything.

At this point all the worry about the mission was gone. His entire focus was on the fight. The only way to come out of this fight alive was to win it, and he had every intention of doing just that, no matter what it took.

A few hundred paces ahead Tex could see a dome-roofed structure, sticking half out of the ground, painted brown to blend into the rocks and sand. The heat shimmered the air above the sand around the dome, giving the entire place the swimming, phantom image of a mirage.

Confederation intelligence had no idea how many Dowers were in that dome, but the maximum number they put it at was seventy. And most of them were men. From all reports, there were no children and few women. Three trained operatives against seventy humans armed only with guns. Tex figured that under normal circumstances, the Dowers wouldn't stand a chance. But he had learned that circumstances were rarely normal.

The Dowers had five orbit-lander spacecraft, all of which were on the ground at the moment in a wide valley on the other side of the base, next to a small repair building. Those ships were heavily armed for space combat and very fast. Seton's orders were for Tex and the team to try to capture the ships after the dome, but if the ships could not be taken, they were to blow up all five of them where they sat.

Tex figured it would be a lot easier just to blow them all up. Luckily for his team, none of the ships had weapons that would work well in the atmosphere. And from what Intel had reported, it would take a good hour for any of them to be scrambled to provide air support for the target. Unless a mission had been planned for the day, those ships weren't going anywhere fast.

Which was why Tex and Rees and Toole were going after the base first. All that was important to Seton was that the ships didn't get away, to be used again in the future. This mission was to permanently ground the Dower raiders. Blowing up those ships was going to be a pleasure Tex would savor later.

"Looks like they've spotted us," Rees said. "About ten of them comin' out the front door."

"A welcoming committee," Tex said. "How nice."

Tex could see them ahead. All were human and carried laser rifles. It seemed Intel had been right about that.

From their positions high in the rocks, Toole and Rees picked off the Dowers like so many sitting ducks. So far Tex hadn't gotten to fire a shot, but he had no doubt that was about to change.

"They're coming out the side door to the west, as well," Toole said through the comm link in Tex's ear. "Maybe ten more."

Some of the Dowers had made it out the front door alive, and they ducked for cover behind rocks. They were now returning fire upward at Toole's position.

Rees began drawing fire, as well, from those

31

along the side. He had to take cover, which allowed even more of the Dowers to get out of the base and into the heat of the day.

Tex watched as at least five more scrambled out and dived for cover. From what Tex could tell, they all carried laser rifles, more than likely stolen from a Confed ship. Some had pistols, but nothing else major.

One of them pointed in Tex's direction.

"They made you, Tex," Rees said as three Dowers madly scrambled to raise their rifles and fire.

"Considerin' that I'm out in the open," Tex said, keeping his pace steady up the center of the sandy canyon, "that didn't take much."

He knew he was just at the outside edge of his mini's range, but as the three aimed their laser rifles at him, he opened up without missing a step. No point in giving them a chance to test his new armor.

The kick of the machine gun in his hand felt familiar, and it charged him with extra strength. Suddenly the heat was gone. The soft sand, the surrounding rock walls, everything.

Only the targets mattered.

The sand in front of the three Dowers exploded, as his aim was slightly low, but he adjusted instantly and the stream of bullets ripped the three apart before they could even duck behind rocks for cover.

He stopped firing and kept walking, keeping

the mini up and aimed in front of him. The main door of the dome was his goal, and he wasn't planning on stopping until he was inside it.

His attack had allowed Toole and Rees more freedom of fire, and they went back to work, picking off any resistance that poked a head from behind a rock.

Tex just kept walking, firing in bursts at anything that showed up as a target or was stupid enough to take aim at him.

He took two Dowers out in one burst, painting the rocks behind them with bright red streaks.

He cut down three more to his right, then swung around, and caught two others on his left.

All the while he kept walking.

His armor deflected a few laser shots, mostly off his lower legs. He had seen combat reports of heavily armored operatives being cut off at the knees by careful laser fire. Reflective armor was, of course, shiny in bright sunlight, and made him a more obvious target, but it was paying for itself right now.

As he strode into the open area around the dome, the ground was suddenly hard under his feet, as if it were a concrete slab covered in wind-blown dust. This base might turn out to be a lot bigger than intelligence had led them to believe, especially if it stretched very far underground.

Four Dowers burst from the front door of the dome and Tex mowed them down, smashing them back against the structure like so many rag dolls thrown by an angry child.

"No more targets in sight," Rees said as the last of Tex's firing echoed over the sand and rocks.

"Agreed," Toole said.

It looked as if all those who had decided to come outside and fight had been taken care of. Maybe thirty at most.

Tex reloaded his machine gun, then made sure it and the one still on his back had not taken any damage. He had the rest of the Dowers still inside to deal with. And that was going to be a different kind of battle.

"I'm goin' in," Tex said.

"Right behind you," Rees said. "Toole, cover our backs."

"Copy that," Toole said.

"Can you read anyone in there?" Tex asked as Rees seemed to materialize beside him.

Rees carried an organic sensor that detected movement and life-forms within a pretty decent range. It could see through rocks and walls.

"None behind the main door. Three or four to the left. Another three to the right."

"Got it," Tex said.

He stopped fifteen paces in front of the main double doors that opened into the dome. He had no intention of going in that way, and Rees and Toole both knew it. Main entrances and most side entrances for places like this had a nasty habit of being booby-trapped. And since no one was posted in the main hallway guarding it, it was perfectly clear that there were some nasty surprises awaiting them there.

He decided the best bet would be to clear some of those traps away and make those inside think the traps might have worked.

He concluded it was time to bring all his firepower to bear, and he hefted the second Branson minigun in his left hand. Wielding two of the huge weapons at once wasn't something even he could sustain for long. Every once in a while circumstances called for it, though, and this looked like as good a time as any.

The two machine guns in his hands kicked as he aimed them at the center of the double door. The stream of armor-penetrating bullets ripped open the door like so much paper, smashing it backward and into bits.

The next moment a large explosion shook the ground and filled the entrance with flames and smoke. The door had been rigged to blow, just as he had expected.

He put one mini away on his back and moved to a position twenty paces to the right of the main door. Rees moved left.

"Directly in front of you," Rees said. "There are three of them."

Tex just nodded and opened fire at the wall, the gun kicking naturally in his hands. Again its kick had a comforting feel, the thunderous sound almost music to his ears.

The wall shattered inward, a hole opening as he cut away the side of the dome to show a large cafeteria-like space on the other side. His firing also cut down the three Dowers who had taken up a position in the room to ambush anyone making it in through the front door and into the main hallway.

"I got this openin'," Rees said.

"Have fun," Tex said as Rees ducked past him and inside, this time moving to the right along the inside wall of the dome.

Tex turned and went past the smoking and destroyed main entrance to a place twenty paces to the left. Then he opened fire again on that wall.

It burst inward, exposing two meeting rooms and more Dowers. They were again surprised at his attack, and he cut down five of them before they returned fire. Tex was just glad the bad guys never seemed to figure out there was more than one way to get into a room.

"They're trying to get out the back," Toole said. "Heading toward their ships."

"Can you cover them?" Rees asked.

Silence.

Then, "They aren't trying anymore," Toole said, her voice a calm and cool answer to Rees' question.

"Copy that," Rees said.

"I'm headed for the main corridor," Tex said, warning Rees to stay back.

Tex stepped through the opening in the side of the dome and opened fire again, blasting through the wall that separated him from the hallway.

Return fire came from the left, in the direction of the center of the dome.

Time for both guns again.

The second mini fit nicely in his left hand as his right took the first. Then he simply stepped into the hall and let his two guns respond to that challenge, spraying everything ahead of him as he went.

"Got your back," Rees said, firing behind Tex at someone Tex had missed along the way.

"Thanks," Tex said, stopping his coverage of the hallway long enough to see if anyone was left alive ahead of him.

The smoke and dust slowly settled as he moved forward. The sound of his machine gun fire seemed to echo longer than natural in the long space. The hallway was a smoking ruin of strange plastic paneling, bullet-torn carpet, and bodies. It ended at some ripped-up double doors that seemed to be hanging on by one hinge each.

Tex put away one gun and headed for them.

"Don't tell me you're actually goin' to use a door?" Rees said.

"Just as a target," Tex said, blasting the remains

of the doors out of his way as he strode forward, stepping over bodies and through the blood.

Beyond the door return fire filled the entrance from three directions.

From what Tex could tell, the room he had entered was huge, taking up most of the space in the center of the dome and extending up to wide windows overhead, letting in the natural light.

It looked like a green park in there, with Earth trees and plants, grass and walkways. There was even a fountain and a few park benches. It was a stark contrast to the red sand and rocks just outside the dome.

As Rees followed him through the ruined doorway, the heaviest fire came from a grove of oak trees to Tex's right. "Let me take care of this," he said to Rees.

"Have fun," Rees said.

Tex stepped into the big space and opened up on those trees with both guns. The rounds he was using could penetrate steel plating and ship's hulls. They went through the three-foot-round tree trunks like they were so much balsa wood.

It took only a single sweep with both guns before the firing stopped there. But as he paused, shots hit him in the back. One staggered him forward, but didn't get through his armor.

What it did do was make him angry.

He turned and sprayed the area where the firing had come from, mowing down everything.

A Dower hiding in some bushes screamed as the bullets ripped into him.

From the doorway Rees had also been firing, surgically picking off anyone who showed his position.

Suddenly the big room full of plants fell silent, like a park after a day of picnicking.

"Rees," Tex said. "Any more targets?"

"Not on this level," Rees said, checking the sensor. "But I got a half dozen right below us. Looks like they're tryin' to set up a defense of some sort in a room down there."

"Get a couple of frags ready," Tex said.

Rees nodded and pulled two grenades from his belt.

Tex aimed his machine gun at the floor and fired, letting his arm and shoulder absorb the kick.

The hole in the floor opened up to about a foot across.

Tex stopped firing and stepped back. Rees flipped the grenades into the hole, and the two of them moved back toward the doorway.

They had taken only three steps when the grenades exploded, sending a geyser of debris upward through the hole Tex had made. The floor shook as if the dome had been hit by a decent-sized earthquake.

Rees checked his organic sensor. "Nothin' left alive in this building."

"You copy that, Toole?" Tex asked.

"I did," Toole said.

"Next stop, the ships," Tex said. "Then we come back here and see what we can find."

"I like that idea," Rees said, smiling.

"Meet you on the east side," Toole said. "Give me two minutes to get into position, and I'll cover you."

"Two it is," Tex said.

Now they had only one more part of the mission to complete. There were five very dangerous spaceships still sitting on the ground east of this dome. And if Tex was right, the remaining Dower forces were going to protect those ships even more furiously than they protected this plant-filled dome they called home.

He reloaded his guns, checked for damage, and then turned to Rees, who was finishing doing the same thing. "Lead the way, scout."

Rees smiled. "Story of my life."

The smoke from the burning warehouse filled the street, swirling around the tops of the three-story buildings. The smell of gunpowder, blood, and burning wood combined in the air to almost cover the sweet, sickening smell of oranges.

Almost.

What seemed like a never-ending stream of Nationalists had flowed from that warehouse and onto the street. All of them were armed with rifles or pistols. Some were fully dressed, others still in nightclothes or shorts.

They had scrambled for any kind of defensive position they could find, often no more than standing behind a thin light pole.

Hawk used a stone bench on the side of the street for cover, her rifle propped across the top of the bench like a stand. She fired smoothly, using single shots at each target, deliberately making sure the shot found its mark.

One Nationalist, a human with a pot gut and dirty red hair, was firing blindly, sticking only his hand and gun above the stone ledge of a staircase. Hawk took his hand off at the wrist.

The guy screamed in pain and stood, jumping up and down, holding his blood-spurting arm. She let him jump once or twice before she put him out of his misery.

Flint did the same kind of shooting from her higher position on the roof. Even with the swirling smoke, Hawk could tell that Flint wasn't missing very often. It was times like these that showed how much machine there was to Flint.

Between the two of them, just about any Nationalist who thought to try to shoot at them died in the attempt.

Rule and Brit were a lot less subtle. They just walked up the middle of the street, their minguns firing so hard and fast that Hawk knew the guns had to be close to overheating. After the first burst of constant fire, the two started taking turns, tag team. One reloaded while the other cut apart anything in their paths that wasn't stone.

In one blast Rule cut down four Nationalists who were unlucky enough at that moment to be lined up, one behind the other, just as Rule fired.

The first Nationalist simply exploded, the second was cut in half, the third went down like a doll, and the fourth was kicked backwards and pinned against a wall.

"Nice shot," Brit said.

Rule laughed as he kept firing and moving forward. "Just using our resources in a conservative manner."

"Yeah, right," Brit said, spinning to cut down three Nationalists racing for cover in a nearby doorway. His shot was slightly low, and he cut off their legs instead of taking them through the body, as he normally did.

Hawk kept on firing single, well-placed shots that found their targets.

Flint did the same.

The street was beginning to look like a charnel house, and the battle seemed as if it was going to wind down soon. The resistance firing had slowed to almost nothing.

Hawk cut down a man stupid enough to poke his head around the edge of the building.

Flint and Hawk both hit another at the same moment as he tried to run for better cover.

Finally the shooting stopped as Flint from her high position took out the last two NRM members cowering against a ground vehicle.

Brit and Rule were standing in the middle of the street, miniguns swinging slowly from side to side as they searched for targets to cut apart.

The fire in the warehouse raged, though the explosions from the armory had lessened some. Shortly the explosions stopped completely, but Hawk could see that the fire was now working its way up the wall toward the roof.

"Three still behind a stone wall to the left," Flint said.

"Got it," Rule answered, yanking two frags out of his belt and lobbing them one right after another down the street and just past the corner of the wall. The two grenades bounced on the hard pavement and rolled to a stop before exploding.

Both Rule and Brit turned their backs and crouched down, bending their heads forward to let the flat of their back armor take any stray shrapnel.

Hawk also ducked just as the two grenades exploded. No point in taking a chance on catching some metal in the face.

"Clear," Flint said a moment later.

That meant that the grenades had done the job on the targets.

There didn't seem to be any more resistance, at least any who were willing to fire on them.

Without leaving her position, Hawk pulled the organic sensor from her belt and checked the street. Only Rule and Flint showed up. She could see city residents cowering in their apartments, but none of them seemed as if they wanted to even get near a window, let alone attack.

Smart folks.

She stood and moved along the wall toward the burning warehouse. According to her readings there were a number of NRM members still inside, alive, most on the main floor. She counted maybe twenty.

There was an alley to the right of the warehouse that led to the street on the other side. Their intelligence showed no door onto that alley, but Hawk figured there had to be some sort of exit. Right now the alley was choked with smoke and debris from the exploded side of the warehouse, but it was still passable.

She turned the organic sensor in that direction and saw five indicators near the other street. She had no idea if they were targets, or just neighbors. They were grouped tightly, and she couldn't see on the organic sensor what they were doing.

"We have approximately twenty inside, most in the basement," Hawk said. "Five possibles down the alley. I need to check out the other side of the warehouse."

Suddenly a white light flashed down the alley. Hawk knew instantly what it was.

"Missile!" she shouted, and dived for the concrete gutter that separated the sidewalk from the street.

She hit the ground hard and flattened herself in the gutter as the world around her exploded. She could feel her back armor taking some hits, and her wrist suddenly stung. The concussion of the nearby explosion made her ears ring.

She wanted to just lie there for an extra instant, but knew that would mean death. She jumped to her feet, moved back so that she had a line of sight down the alley, and began picking off the targets as they started to load and launch another missile.

Five quick shots at long range.

Five slaps as bodies slammed into walls or the ground.

The missile launcher clanged to the street with the echoes of her last shot.

She then turned around to see how Brit and Rule were doing. What she saw chilled her to the bone.

Both were dead.

It looked as if the missile had exploded right between them, not more than a meter from each. She had been a good ten meters away and had taken some pretty heavy damage. No armor could protect an operative from an almost direct hit from a Thermalite missile.

"Rule and Brit are down," she said.

"I know," Flint said, her voice level. More than

likely she had seen the entire thing from the vantage point of her sniper perch. "We're not coming back this way. Can you retrieve their chips? I have you covered."

Hawk stared at the two bodies. Both had been torn up pretty badly.

The chips Flint had mentioned were the memory chips implanted in seasoned and valuable Confed operatives. They contained event-memory records of the past thirty days of an operative's life, and a record of the skills and knowledge they had developed throughout their lifetimes. When retrieved from a battlefield casualty and then implanted into a cloned physical replica of the operative, the chips made it possible for the Confed to field a close facsimile of a valuable, deceased operative within days of its predecessor's demise.

As long as the chip was recovered intact, its memories would become part of the new clone's brain. The chips weren't perfect, and they generally left an operative with memory gaps, usually of childhood and personal details, but it allowed the operative to continue doing the work the Confed needed done.

Hawk wasn't sure how she felt about the chips. The fact that she had one of her own was something she was always aware of. And full-body cloning wasn't something she much liked. But if it could bring back Brit and Rule, she'd live with her doubts.

Hawk pulled out the slender, clawlike tool needed to extract the chips, but then at a glance she could tell there would be no recovering either Brit's or Rule's chips. Their heads had been shattered and made worthless by the intense closeness of the explosion. She could see part of one chip sticking out of a part of Rule's exposed brain.

"No recovery possible," Hawk said after bending over what was left of Brit's head.

"Oh," was all Flint said in reply.

Brit and Rule were gone for good. It was a price every operative understood. But Hawk was relatively new to operations. This was the first time she had lost a team member.

She didn't like the feeling. It made her angry.

And right now she had some NRM survivors to take that anger out on.

Chapter Three

Local law enforcement's authority and jurisdiction in local affairs is absolute, one of the bedrock principles of the Confederation of Allied Worlds. That's why we don't talk to the locals.

—J. I. Graf,
Protectorate Secretary of Policy and
Practices, in a memo to
Regional Office managers

Tex strode from the green world of Dower dome out into the dry heat of the red desert. Sweat formed almost instantly on his face and hands and evaporated just as quickly. After being in the cool, green-filled dome, it seemed much hotter outside now than it had been just a few minutes ago. The orange sun of this system was large in the sky over the hills to the east, baking everything.

He stood and waited for the clear signal from Toole, studying the area in front of him. A road led from the door of the dome toward the airfield, where the spaceships were parked. It was packed hard, and his boots didn't sink into it like they had in the sand.

A shallow hill separated the dome from the landing area, more than likely to protect the dome from any wash from the engines when taking off and landing. The road curved through a small pass at the crest of the hill. From where he stood just outside the dome, he could not see any of the ships.

He had managed to pick up a really nice Thermalite missile launcher that had been carried by one of the escaping Dowers when he was shot just inside the dome. Running low on minigun ammo, he ditched one of them, and the launcher was now mounted on his back in the empty slot, checked and ready to use.

"In position," Toole said.

She had taken up a sniper location in the mound of rocks to the right of the pass leading over the small rise. From there she could see anything coming at them on the path or trying to circle around and back to the dome.

Tex stepped out toward the ships, keeping his pace measured and set, his gun aimed forward. He had no doubt they would meet more resistance. The Dowers lifelines, their very lives, were those five heavily armed spaceships. But Tex was certain the Dowers hadn't foreseen a ground attack that wouldn't give those ships the time needed to get into space. The ships' weapons were mostly useless against an assault coming while they were parked and powered down. And

Tex and the team had every intention of taking advantage of that.

"Ships in sight?" Rees asked Toole.

He had scrambled up the left hill, moving from rock to rock to get to the ridge line.

Tex just used the road, his machine gun aimed forward, fully loaded and ready to fire.

"Two hundred meters in front of me," Toole said. "I count a dozen defenders on the ground around the ships."

"I'm in position now," Rees said. "Organic sensor shows no others hidin' in the rocks. Let's do some pickin'."

"Copy that," Toole said.

Tex was still a good hundred paces from where the road crested over the slight rise and went down to the ships. He could see the top of one, but that was all.

Toole's and Rees' individual shots echoed in the heat and thin air, and were quickly answered by return fire. But the amount of return fire didn't seem to Tex to be enough for the number of Dowers that had escaped to the ships. More than likely they had taken shelter inside the ships and were still hoping to get launched in time. If he had anything to say about it, that wasn't going to happen.

Tex glanced at his mission read-outs. Their attack, from first sniper shot to now, had been under way for a total of only eleven minutes. Not even close to enough time to power up a ship and make an emergency liftoff.

He reached a point where he could see over the top of the small hill and stopped to let Toole and Rees finish off their single-shot work. With his miniguns, there wasn't much he could do at this distance. Better to let the sharpshooters have all the fun.

Though approximately the same size, the five ships were of all different shapes. They sat on the sand like alien statues, very out of place, glinting in the hot sun. Three were on their sides, and two, sitting on their tail assemblies, noses pointed skyward. All five ships were human-built, Tex was sure, but from the designs, they were clearly from different systems.

All the ships had been stolen over the last few years, and from what intelligence had told them, they were armed with both human and alien weapons. All were painted matte black and looked threatening just sitting on the red sand. He could only imagine what they might look like to a cargo ship captain in deep space as they swarmed around his defenseless vessel.

"They're moving a ship-board laser," Rees said. "Second ship on the right."

"Got it," Toole said. "I'll take the shot."

It was clear to Tex from the bodies lying on the hard-packed sand around the base of the ships that Toole and Rees had done their jobs, one shot

after another. Any Dower that had remained outside a ship was now dead.

And now those inside one ship were taking a
huge chance at firing a laser cannon designed for
space combat. Without the ship's natural space-
borne shields up and in position, the cannon had
no protection from return fire.

Tex stood on the top of the ridge and waited as
the laser swung toward them from the right.
Then, just as it pointed at Toole's position, she
fired.

The sound of her single shot echoed over the
sand and rocks and died off.

"Looks good," she reported.

Tex watched and waited. Around him the silence of the desert seemed to intensify.

A direct hit meant her shot, aimed precisely,
had gone straight down the four-inch-wide barrel
of the laser cannon and smashed into the power
coils inside. Tex knew exactly what would happen next.

The ship rocked violently as the huge laser
cannon exploded, the shell of the ship keeping almost all the force inside. The explosion, muffled,
sounded like distant thunder.

"Oh, that's got to hurt," Rees said. Then he
added, "Nice shootin'."

"Thanks," Toole said.

"Yeah, real nice," Tex said, shaking his head
in amazement. That kind of shot didn't happen

every day. He knew, without a doubt, that ship was never going to get off the ground again. The explosion of that laser had been contained inside and would have instantly killed anyone on board.

"We have a second idiot movin' a laser," Rees said. "Round ship, three back. Laser is rotating around from my side. I got the shot."

Tex could see exactly what Rees was talking about.

As the laser barrel swung around, Rees fired.

"Missed," he said.

An instant later the laser fired, low and to the left of Rees' position. Rock exploded, and Tex ducked away, letting his back armor take the impact of the small flying shards.

"Second ship in line has one moving," Toole said.

"These folks aren't real smart," Rees said. He fired again, the bullet pinging off the hull of the ship.

Tex knew without Rees' having to say a word that it was another miss. And then the laser had moved to a position where neither Rees nor Toole had a clear shot.

Time for some heavy work. Tex slung his machine gun over his shoulder and lined up the launcher he had picked up in the dome.

"I'll give you some cover," Tex said, firing the missile.

The Thermalite missile exploded in the sand at

the base of the second ship, right where Tex aimed it, sending a cloud of sand and dust into the air.

Under the cloud's cover, Rees sprinted down the side of the hill and in under the second ship, which stood with its nose pointed skyward. With a quick snap, he planted what Tex knew to be a penetrating charge, clamping it against a thruster right under the ship's engine.

Rees made a dash for the rocks as the laser from the third ship in line fired, missing Rees, but peppering him with rock chips.

A moment later the charge detonated, and the explosion rocked the upright ship.

For a moment Tex thought the ship might actually topple over like a tree falling to the ground. Then it righted itself as a second explosion inside the ship sent the hull plating buckling outward.

"Uh-oh," Toole said. "Rees, get out of there!"

Tex instantly saw what she meant. A third explosion bulged another part of the ship's skin. And then a few seconds later a fourth, lower and to the right.

"Oh, no!" Toole shouted as Rees made it back to his old position.

Toole and Tex knew exactly what was happening, but Tex couldn't believe it. The idiots inside that ship, in hopes of getting power more quickly to the weapons, had hooked the laser weapons up in a direct circuit to the ship's engine reactor core.

When Rees set off the explosion under the engine, it created a feedback loop that was working itself from laser to laser and then back to the core.

At this point there was no one alive on that ship to stop it.

"It's cascading!" Tex shouted.

He turned and took two running steps back down the road in the direction of the dome, then dived full out, hoping to get back over the crest of the hill far enough for a little protection.

One more small explosion from inside the ship echoed through the air as he hit the ground and rolled downslope.

Maybe, just maybe, they would get lucky, and the ship's core wouldn't explode, maybe one of the explosions would stop the cascade.

He pressed himself into the sand as far as he could.

Suddenly the world flashed bright white, and the ground slammed up into him like a giant fist against his entire body.

The fist then clasped his body and squeezed.

The rocket launcher was ripped from his grasp. The mini was torn off his back like so much frayed cloth.

His back armor turned hot, then hotter. His skin was burning, but he didn't dare move, turn over, or even breathe.

A blast furnace opened above his prone body. He fought to hold his breath in the choking dust and sand that buffeted him. He kept his eyes clenched and he did what he could with his armored arm to protect his face.

Under him the hard-packed road turned to fine sand as the ground shook. The sand seemed to melt, become liquid, pulling him down like a man sinking in a pool.

The world tilted and spun. The heat baked into him.

Then the wind hit, rushing back into the vacuum created by the explosion, trying to drag him over the hill.

With one arm protecting his face, he spread out the other, holding on, pressing himself down into the sand as much as he could as the hurricane-force winds ripped at his armor and back and legs.

Then, almost as quickly as it had happened, it was over.

The winds eased.

Then stopped.

The ground stopped trembling.

He lay there, facedown, hurting in more places than he could have imagined.

His ears were ringing, making his world sound like too many alarms were going off at the same time.

He wanted to just lie there, but he didn't dare.

First he took a breath of the hot, dusty air.

No problem there, except that the simple act of breathing told him the skin on his back was burnt badly.

He moved slowly, carefully, testing his body. No bones seemed to be broken, but his face was also burnt. With each movement, the intense pain made him sure that his back and legs had severe burns under his armor.

And since the core of that engine had been a tiny, highly efficient fusion reactor, there was no doubt he was going to need radiation treatments—and fairly soon. In effect, he had the worst possible sunburn.

He eased up into a sitting position, spitting sand from his mouth and trying to work his eyes open carefully to not scratch them with all the sand.

What slowly emerged around him as his vision cleared was a sight he could have imagined only in a nightmare. The ground along the top of the ridge had been scoured clean, and the area surrounding the blast had fused into glass. He had been lucky to be just over the ridge; that was for sure.

He stood and almost blacked out from the pain.

He braced himself, took a deep breath, and then closed his eyes. Then with more deep breaths of the hot air, he willed the pain back. The spinning stopped, and again he opened his eyes, focusing himself on the task of regulating his breathing as he looked around.

Most of the Dower dome had simply vanished, leaving only some remains of walls and green plants sitting on what had been a foundation and flooring, now exposed to the hot sun. The rock-walled valley they had landed in was gone, filled with sand and debris.

"Rees? Toole? Report."

No answer.

His comm system might be broken. Or theirs. He didn't want to think about the other, more likely option.

Toward the ships the hill had been polished clean from the blast. The pile of rocks where Toole had been was gone.

Tex eased himself one step at a time toward the ridgeline.

In the valley that had been filled with five suborbital ships and sand, nothing but scraps of melted metal remained. In the distance he could see a fairly large pile of rubble that he figured must be the wreckage of one or two of the ships tangled together. But that was a good kilometer away.

Rees had been hiding among rocks to Tex's left. Those rocks were also gone, and there was no sign of him either.

"Toole?" Tex repeated, starting slowly toward her last known location, ignoring the pain of each step.

"Rees?"

He glanced back at where he had dived for

cover. He had made it over the ridgeline when the ship's core reactor blew. There was no doubt that had saved him, sending most of the blast over his head.

But Toole and Rees had both been on top of the ridge.

He had seen ships' cores explode before, but always in space. And always from a pretty good distance and behind the protection of another ship's screens and shields. He couldn't imagine living through one this close, on the ground, yet somehow he had. He just hoped Toole and Rees would be as lucky.

He painfully made his way to Toole's last position, the burns on his back and legs bleeding and sweating in the hot sun. He was going to need help soon; of that, there was no doubt.

He flicked the switch on his secure comm system. "Dower op ship, come in."

"Go ahead," their pilot's voice said.

"Mission accomplished," Tex said. "Come on in."

"Copy that," the pilot said. "What happened? I'm a hundred kilometers away, and I got bounced out of my chair."

"A Dower ship's core exploded," Tex said. "I need help searchin' for the other two operatives."

"On my way," the pilot said, and cut the connection.

Tex nodded to himself. The pilot was good. He

would be here and on the ground in under a minute.

Tex reached the place where Toole had been. Nothing but bare, almost polished stone.

He put his back to the spot where the ship had been and started walking away from it, over the hill. Within twenty steps he was back among rocks and debris that had been kicked over the hill by the force of the blast.

He slowly worked his way down the hill, painfully turning one way and then another, careful to make sure he didn't miss anything.

Toole's only hope would have been to get over the ridge as he had done. If she had simply ducked and hoped to use the stones as cover, he doubted he'd find anything left of her.

Twenty more paces, and he found his answer. Parts of Toole's fancy new armor and some flesh and bones were jumbled together. Her head had been smashed into a shape far larger than it should be, and both her legs were gone.

Tex pulled the memory chip claw from his pocket. If he got her chip, she could be cloned and brought back. But the part of Toole's head where the chip had been was completely missing.

He looked around her body, hoping to find the black square of the chip's housing, without luck.

She was gone for good.

Tex turned away, forcing himself to keep

moving. There was still a chance that Rees had gotten back over the ridge and was only injured.

"Rees?" Tex called over the communication link.

No answer.

The ship flashed overhead, the rush of the engines filling the scene of destruction and breaking the silence that slowly had replaced the ringing in his ears. The ship turned quickly and settled onto the sand near the remains of the Dower dome.

Tex did the same thing in Rees' search as he had done for Toole. He went back to the last place he saw Rees, put his back to the explosion site, and started down the hill.

The pilot, breaking standard practice, left the ship, jumped to the sand, and started toward Tex. When he was a hundred paces away, he shouted, "The organic sensor shows only you surviving here."

Tex nodded. "No one under the dome floor?"

"No," the pilot said. He started up the hill toward Tex and then suddenly stopped.

"Here," he said, his voice barely working.

He pointed down at something in the rocks and then turned away, heading back toward the ship. He was clearly upset with what he had found.

Tex moved slowly down to where the pilot had indicated, among some piled rocks rolled there by the blast. What little bit of Rees' body that was left, was jammed into a crevice between two boulders.

Tex looked at the bloody, sand-covered mess until he could make some sense of it. Part of the torso, one leg, part of an arm, and only part of a head. Not the part with the chip.

Rees was gone for good, as well.

This mission had cost Confed two top operatives. Tex hoped it was worth it.

The pilot was about to get back on the ship when Tex stopped him. "Not yet. I need help."

"I'm not recovering those bodies," the pilot said, shaking his head.

"Not that," Tex said. "I need help gettin' into the basement area that was under the dome. I'm not ending this mission with two dead and nothin' to show for it."

The pilot nodded. "Copy that. But first I'll get a medkit. You look like you need it."

"Thanks," Tex said as the pilot ducked inside the ship.

The pilot's comment allowed the pain he had been holding back to rise to the surface again. It rode up inside him, letting him feel the burns on his back and legs, his torn skin, sand-blasted eyes. He pushed it all away again, refusing to acknowledge it yet, and started down the shallow hill toward the ship, moving slowly.

But at least he was still moving.

* * *

Hawk looked at the open front door of the NRM warehouse, studying her organic sensor to see where her targets were located. Rule's and Brit's bodies were still lying in the middle of the street, and there they would remain. There was nothing on them to lead the local authorities back to Confed. Operatives carried no identification of any kind on any mission. If somehow the memory chip fell into the wrong hands, no conventional law enforcement agency—or any agency, for that matter, knew what it was.

Every op knew there would be no burial service, or medals. If you lived, you were rewarded. If you didn't, sometimes your body stayed right where it fell, waiting for someone else to clean up the mess. Those were the rules, and Hawk understood them. On missions there was seldom time to worry about taking care of the dead. Especially when the mission wasn't yet finished.

"Only ten targets left inside," Hawk said to Flint, who was still holding a sniper's post on top of one of the buildings.

"I'll go around to the other side," Flint said

"Copy that," Hawk said. "How long?"

"Seventy count," Flint said, already on the move, judging from the sound of her voice.

Hawk knew they had only one course of action left now that Brit and Rule were dead. She had to go inside and see what she could see in full stealth mode. Flint would get around to a new position to provide cover if Hawk needed it.

In the distance came the first sounds of sirens. Locals would be here in a minute or two. She paused and looked back.

Nothing moved around her.

Pulling out two incendiary grenades, she rolled them toward Rule's and Brit's bodies and then stepped back behind a stone wall for cover. The explosion rocked the street.

She glanced back at what was left of the two ops. Nothing but charred remains. No one would trace them to Confed now. Better safe than sorry.

She waited the seventy count, watching for any sign of life along the body-lined street between the two buildings. The smell of blood, the Thermalite from the NRM missile, and the still burning corner of the warehouse mixed with the orange smell, making the air seem unbelievably thick. Hawk wanted more than anything else to just get away from this place.

Out of this smell.

But there was still a mission to finish, and she was going to finish it.

"In position," Flint reported.

Hawk started to move toward the open door. Still twenty paces away, she took a frag grenade from her belt and tossed it inside, turning her back as the explosion ripped the hallway. That was just in case anyone had set any traps.

The explosion set off nothing else.

She went into stealth mode and ducked in through the door, keeping to the wall on her left, her Powerblade out and ready in case someone stumbled into her way.

After a short hall, she entered the main area of the warehouse. The space rose three stories high, and from what she could see through the smoke from the corner fire, it was filled with equipment, ground transports, and high piles of boxes. A couple of burnt bodies were sprawled on the smooth concrete floor, more than likely tossed there from the armory explosion.

That area to her right was still burning, flames climbing the wall next to a catwalk suspended ten meters over her head. The catwalk ran the entire distance of the large interior space, with a large number of doors leading off of it.

The flames gave the smoke an orange look, complementing the smell of this wretched planet.

She paused against the wall, using a panel truck for cover as she checked her organic sensor to see where her targets were. Two were crouched under another truck not more than thirty paces to her left. More than likely they were waiting, hoping to surprise whoever came in. Four more were scattered around the room.

Wouldn't they be surprised to know she had walked right past them while they waited for the police?

For no apparent reason, one man swung around and fired in a panic at a window, breaking it out. That firing brought up some more rifle fire from around the room, but she didn't bother worrying about it. They weren't aiming at her, since they couldn't see her.

She stayed in stealth, frozen in place, as they wasted their ammunition into the hood and panel of the truck, through the windows, and at the walls.

Then she started up the stairs toward the balcony just as one guy grunted when a stray shot ripped through him. He tipped forward, landing with a loud clang on the catwalk.

A woman wearing a green overall uniform like a mechanic might wear jumped from a doorway and opened fire on the main entrance, as if there were anything there to fire at. These people were really spooked, and they were jumping at shadows. Considering what she and her team had done to them, that made sense for a bunch of amateurs.

Hawk, her sensor on, moved along the wall, checking out the rooms, studying the trucks, trying to find any spoils that might be worthwhile. She knew that nothing she was going to find would be worth the lives of two ops, but she would be damned if she was going to leave empty-handed.

It took her two full minutes to move carefully

around the upper section before she was convinced it was clean.

"Open for business," Hawk said into her comm link. "I'm going into one of the offices."

"Copy that," Flint said. "We're getting local company out here. Will you be able to get to the roof?"

"Not a problem," Hawk said, glancing over to make sure the stairs were still where they were supposed to be. "The targets still alive in here will hold off the locals. Call in our ride. Give me three minutes, tops."

Over the link, Hawk heard Flint call for the ship to land on the roof of the warehouse and retrieve them. From the time the ship landed until the time it took off, they would have had no more than fifteen minutes. But fifteen minutes was a long time in this business. More than enough time to clean out some of this now-defunct organization's treasury.

More than enough time to die, as well.

Chapter Four

Some call for tolerance toward this "Sword of Shadoon" cult—dialogue, respect for their beliefs. Bah! They are nothing short of a menace to everything the Confed holds dear!

—Carson Barnes,
Cygnus V delegate,
in an address to the Quorum

Tex yanked debris from the clogged stairway that led from the surface down into the basement area of what was left of the Dower dome. His every movement hurt, but not so much as it would have done twenty minutes before.

The medkit had some pain pills and burn spray, and he had peeled off the last of his ruined armor, which allowed him to move without having the burns rubbed. In a number of places the armor had taken skin with it, but he had managed the pain, and now he was digging for anything of value he could take back with them. It was a part of the mission he had to finish. He knew Rees and Toole would have done the same thing if he were lying out there in the sun, blasted apart by a spaceship's engine core.

The fact that he couldn't bring their chips back

nagged at him. He had grown used to having the chip in his head. He had grown used to having that security blanket, knowing that even if he did stop a bullet, he might return. But having chips in their heads hadn't done Rees or Toole any good at all. They were dead, and no amount of modern science was going to bring them back.

Tex made himself stop thinking about them and focus on the task at hand.

He felt odd, even naked, still being on the ground, in the middle of a mission, without at least one mini strapped over his shoulder. But at the moment the burns on his back and arms wouldn't allow it. He had taken a laser rifle from the ship's supply and carried it to the edge of the ruined dome, where he stood it against a rock. Not much firepower by his standards, but he felt better having a solid weapon close at hand.

He had also taken a Black Pistol from the ship and stuck it in his belt, along with a few frag grenades and a flashlight. He never carried a pistol. They were too small and not worth the effort, but for this once, he needed something that left his hands free. Having it felt better than having nothing going down into that basement.

He finally got enough junk out of the way so that he could get down the stairs and into the wide hallway below. Once he hit the bottom he could see that the hall ended in the remains of a freight elevator. There were six large doors leading off the hallway, and a type of wheeled forklift parked against one side. There were enough holes in the floor above so that he didn't even need to turn on the flashlight.

The pilot had agreed to stay on the surface, inside his craft, and keep watch, using the radar, organic detector, and conventional visuals. They maintained constant contact, so that Tex wouldn't have any surprise visits while in the confined space underground.

Tex shoved open the first door on the left at the bottom of the stairs and was greeted by a large weapons cache. Rifles, miniguns, missile launchers, flamethrowers, boxes of grenades, laser cannons, and even a couple of particle beam cannons. Heavy duty.

He walked a few steps into the large storage area and did a slow inspection. Most of the weapons were used, clearly taken in raids. Some had been restored, and there were boxes of parts in the rear of the room. It was a decent find, but there wasn't much of anything worth his time hauling to the ship, except maybe the particle beam cannons.

He moved those out into the hallway and stood them against the wall; then he looked the room over one more time. Nothing was worth carrying out, especially in his condition. Maybe during the mission he'd have used some of this, but now it wasn't worth the effort. Still, a single timed charge on his way out would make sure no one else used these weapons against the Confed.

The next door down the hall led to an empty room, as did the first one on the right side.

"Still clear out here," the pilot reported. "Anything worth taking down there?"

"Nothin' much so far," Tex said as he tried—and failed—to shove open the next door. He knew that in addition to all the items the Dower had stolen, they had access to large amounts of cash converted from fencing stolen goods on a half dozen planets. But the question was, had all that money been stored down here, or had it vanished in the explosion?

"Too bad," the pilot said.

"Hang on," Tex said. "I got a locked door here."

So far this was the only one that had been locked. A large timber had fallen into the old freight elevator, and he yanked it free, swinging it around so that its blunt end was in front of him. Then bracing himself, he swung it at the door.

The impact jarred his sore hands and sent shooting pains through his back and arms.

The door didn't open. Solid thing, and he didn't feel like injuring himself more by pounding on it.

"Goin' to have to blow this one," Tex said, warning the pilot so he wouldn't be worried about an explosion.

"Copy that," the pilot said.

Tex glanced over his shoulder at the staircase to

make sure it was still clear; then he dropped two grenades at the base of the door and turned and ran as fast as his burnt skin and sore muscles would take him.

He was back up and into the hot sun when the grenades went off.

"You need some help?" the pilot asked as the dust shot out of a dozen openings and more of the ceiling fell into the hallway.

"I'll let you know in a minute," Tex said, heading back down the stairs into the dust- and smoke-filled basement. The once-locked door had been blown inward. It now hung on one hinge like a leaf about to drop from a limb.

Inside the room, the sight that greeted him made him whistle long and low.

"What?" the pilot asked.

"Bring some packs and other carry bags," Tex said. "We just hit the mother lode."

"On my way," the pilot said, the excitement clear in his voice. Like operatives, pilots got a cut of the profits on a mission because they risked their own lives and their own ships. Tex and the pilot had just gotten a lot wealthier.

Tex moved slowly into the room, his pistol out and ready. There were a number of bodies below a hole that gaped in the ceiling. They had been the ones he had killed on his first pass through the dome. One slow walk around the twenty-pace square room convinced him no Dower was left alive and that there were no traps of any kind waiting for him.

Next he went to work slowly checking the boxes of currency stacked neatly in the middle of the room. He examined each one in turn to make sure none of them were booby-trapped.

The currency he could see on the top of the stack had to be from twenty different worlds, and there was a substantial amount of Confed script, as well. There was no telling what else was stored in the lower boxes. The stack was six feet tall and an even greater distance across. And that wasn't all. . . .

"Wow!" the pilot said as he stumbled over the rubble and into the room. "This bunch was loaded."

"That they were," Tex said. "Nice of them to package it for us, all nice and neat."

"Real nice," the pilot said as he dropped the bags he had been carrying. He picked up two boxes of bills from the Dankin system and headed for the door.

"Might want to move the ship in closer so that the hatch is almost at the top of the stairs," Tex said. "And each time we go into the ship with a load, we check the sensors for approaching traffic. Both of us."

"Good thinking," the pilot said, and vanished out into the hallway.

The money they had found here was going to

set Tex up for a long time, and it would fund a lot of other operations for Confed. Of that he had no doubt. But it wasn't the money that really had his interest. It was the dozen golden statues he had spotted crowded on a shelf on the back wall.

He moved closer, again making sure nothing was booby-trapped. The statues appeared to be Seer figures, decorated with some sort of elaborate religious iconography. The Seers were an alien race that had scattered colonies throughout the Known Worlds. They were supposed to have fantastic psychic abilities. Tex had never met a Seer in the flesh, but the statues' features were unmistakable.

He had heard rumors of a Seer colony that followed a fanatical leader known as Shadoon. The colony was starting to worry some people in the Confed. Tex had no doubt that at some point, operatives like him would be dealing with that colony.

In the briefing for this mission, Tex had learned that certain religious artifacts had been taken from a Sword of Shadoon ship about three months ago. It had caused quite a stir, since the Confed didn't want the followers of Shadoon getting any more angry and militant than they already were.

The Shadoon had blamed the Confed and its Protectorate, and sympathetic Seer delegates in the Quorum had taken the podium to rail against this latest trampling of the rights and sovereignty of nonhuman races.

Protectorate officials had pointed out that, given the method and location of the attack, it had most likely been the work of the Dowers, but the Seers then claimed the Dowers were merely a front for Protectorate-sponsored exploitation of nonhumans. The matter still boiled.

Tex had heard that the theft of the statues had been one of the main reasons operations had decided to move on the Dowers.

The reason Tex was here.

Tex picked up one statue and was stunned by how heavy it was. "For something so small, you pack a lot of weight and problems," he said out loud to the golden figure as he inspected its strange design.

It looked like some sort of weird mantislike alien cross between an insect and a bird. Tex turned it over in his hands, staring intently at the alien form. He had never seen anything like it before. He held it up to see it in better light. There was no doubt in his mind these were the Shadoon statues, worth a fortune.

But no matter what they were worth, they sure were freakish-looking things. And they gave him the creeps.

"Nothing so far," Flint reported to Hawk.

Hawk was going in and out of stealth mode,

conserving energy as she worked her way from one room to another along the balcony level overlooking the large, smoke-filled warehouse. The Nationalists idiots had stopped firing at every shadow, and they were now yelling back and forth, trying to figure out how to deal with the local police. Hawk had no doubt that they were in a fix on that score.

"I'm almost to the roof," Flint said. "The locals are here in force. The ship in two minutes."

"Copy that," Hawk said. Then ahead of her she saw what she had been looking for. A door with an extra lock, and visible reinforcement.

It took her less than ten seconds to get to the door. The stairs up to the roof were only fifty paces from the door she was facing. If this was in fact the treasury, it would be fairly easy to get some of it up to the ship.

The smoke at this level was thicker, and it stung Hawk's eyes. If the fire kept growing at this rate, the building wouldn't last much longer than she was going to stay.

Hawk glanced at her read-outs. They were ten minutes and thirty seconds into the operation. The police and emergency response teams would be occupied with the bodies in the street for a while, and the remaining live targets would slow them down even more. So the locals would not be a factor as long as they hadn't brought air support.

The door was locked, and it took Hawk a long twenty-one seconds to get it open. It took even less time to scan the room and access what she found.

No treasury.

No safe.

Nothing.

"How stupid is this?" Hawk said as she did a quick walk around the room.

"What's wrong?" Flint asked over the comm link.

"Someone must have tipped them we were coming and cleaned out what looked to be a treasury." Hawk moved back to a spot on the catwalk and stared through the swirling smoke. It was making her eyes hurt more with each passing minute. And she had no doubt it was causing her to be more visible even in stealth mode. The fire was clearly expanding.

"On the roof," their pilot's voice said. "The building is surrounded by locals. East corner is completely engulfed in fire. I don't want to stay parked here too long."

"Copy that," Flint said. "Hawk, I've got you covered when you're ready."

"I'm going to check one more room," Hawk said.

She ducked down the walkway and into the office. Maybe Brit and Rule had blown it up when they blew the armory. She had only a minute to find out. And this warehouse was so big, a good search wasn't going to be possible.

The office had two desks and a door that led to another office with a much nicer desk. It looked like some sort of executive office. None of the outer office files were locked, and she only glanced at them. She broke open the lock of the inner office file with a single kick and rifled through the useless paperwork she found there. At a glance she could guess this paperwork was going to cause some problems for local politicians, but there was nothing of value to her.

Only the lower desk drawer remained to be broken open, as well.

"Any luck?" Flint asked.

"Nothing," Hawk said as she yanked open the drawer. More files. One folder in the back labeled SHADOON caught her attention, and she opened it. It showed payment arrangements between NRM bank accounts and Shadoon accounts.

"Weird," she said out loud.

"What?" Flint asked over the comm link.

"Aren't the Shadoon that cult, those Seers in the . . . Ulysses system?" Hawk asked.

"They are," Flint said.

"So what kind of business would they have with a local militant organization?"

Flint said nothing for a moment, then answered, "That's a question we might not want to ask of the wrong people."

Hawk knew exactly what Flint meant. An operative getting involved in any kind of politics in the Confed was generally considered a bad career move.

"Getting a little warm up here," the pilot said.

"On my way," Hawk answered.

Hawk shoved the file back in the drawer and headed for the roof. No treasury to take back with them, but at least they had accomplished their primary objective of shutting down the NRM. She doubted that the NRM organization would be causing any troubles for the Confed embassy anytime soon.

Pity the mission had cost two operatives. But she knew it was the risk they all took. It could just as easily have been her lying out there on the street, dead for the better interests of the Confederation of Allied Worlds.

"Oh, man, the Shadoon statues!" the pilot said, coming back into the room and moving up beside Tex as he held up one of the heavy gold figures. "Commander Seton is going to *love* seeing us coming."

"That he is," Tex said, putting the statue he had been holding into a bag and starting to load the others. There was no doubt that the return of these would generate cash as well as some political points for the higher-ups.

Now they had to get them loaded and get off this godforsaken planet.

Tex made ten painful trips to the ship, loading first the statues and then large parts of the Dower treasury. Then he turned his attention to the two large doors in this basement he still hadn't opened.

He stopped at the one closest to the bottom of the staircase and kicked the door in. The room was food storage, mostly bulk goods and stacks of basics like protein packs and fiber supplements. The walls were covered with shelves of food and drink, and the entire back area was filled with bottled water. There was enough in that large room to feed an army, which was what it had been doing. A hole in the roof of the room showed where the supply elevator had led up to a kitchen area in the now vanished dome.

The middle door off the hallway was unlocked and led into a very large room, more than twice the size of the food storage area or treasury vault. It was full of desks and filing cabinets and computers. Some of the cabinets were labeled with a planet's name, including one for Wren. This confirmed what Intel had reported in its briefings, that the Dowers were linked into the business networks of a number of worlds. It was no wonder the Dowers seemed to always know when an important cargo was being moved through their area.

Tex moved over and pulled open a drawer. Records, purchase orders, nothing more.

He went from cabinet to cabinet, opening one drawer after another, glancing at the paperwork and file titles.

After a few minutes it became clear that the Dowers had operated like a large business. There had been five different owners, one for each of the five spaceships. Each owner took care of his own crew and took a cut of everything they got in a raid.

It was also clear they had agents on many of the nearby worlds and a much larger payroll than would account for the number of people killed here. He took what information he felt would be needed to find the agents and stuffed it in a pocket.

In one drawer, Tex pulled out a piece of paper showing the original Dower agreement. The name Dower even came from the five ship-owners' names: Daniels, Owens, Webber, Evert, and Rankin.

Tex wondered which one of them had been stupid enough to order the laser link into the core engine. It didn't much matter now, since they were all dead.

Tex was about to close the last drawer when a key caught his attention. The key had been hung on the inside of the file drawer, and he wouldn't have seen it if he hadn't been standing to the side. It didn't fit that drawer.

He held up the key and looked at it, then at the locks on the other file cabinets. It clearly didn't fit any of them. Or any drawers in any of the desks. But yet somewhere that key fit something important.

Tex took the key and moved back out into the hallway to check the door he had blasted open into the vault room. It wasn't a fit.

"You find any locked boxes?" Tex asked the pilot as he came in for another load of currency.

"Nope," the pilot said, looking at the key. It was somewhat longer than a normal key, with a type of flange you didn't tend to see except in high security areas, or government offices.

Tex shrugged and was about to put the key into his pocket when the pilot said, "I used to work in an office, clerking, while I got my flight certification. Let me see if I can spot anything in that business office that thing might fit."

Tex handed him the key and then followed him into the room with all the desks and file cabinets.

"Where did you find it?" the pilot asked.

Tex showed him the drawer, and the pilot went and stood in front of the cabinet, looking around. Then he laughed and moved over to what looked like a wooden table used for conference meetings.

"Fake wood," he said, knocking on the top of the table. "See how thick this corner is?"

Tex stared closely at the table, finally seeing what the pilot meant. The large table was designed so that an area in the center of each side was thick, dividing the space under the table into four quarters. It was a design that had been around since before Tex was born and now looked old.

"This center area often hid a secret file," the pilot said. He knelt down and looked under the edge of the table, then inserted the key, and turned it.

The wood facing on the table stand opened, and a drawer rolled out.

The pilot sort of ruffled through the papers and shrugged. "Nothing. I'll take another load to the ship." The pilot flipped Tex the key and headed for the door.

Tex nodded and picked up the papers, scanning through them quickly. Most of it was nothing more than personal agreements between the five partners, until he got to a series of messages, clearly copied down for nothing more than reference. It outlined an agreement between the Dower and the Sword of Shadoon. It seemed they were sharing information, wealth, and were in the process of negotiating for the statues.

Tex was stunned. How extensive was the cult of Shadoon? This clearly indicated that the cult was far bigger than he had heard. Of course, he was only an operative. He wasn't generally kept in the political loop for information of this sort. But he would wager a large number of people up the line above him would find this file very interesting.

He was about to put the file under his arm and go to take another load to the ship when he spotted a holo disk. Directly under the Shadoon notes was a holo disk marked with the notation D. PETRIE.

Tex stared at the name, half expecting it to change.

It didn't.

It could be anyone, but the only Petrie Tex knew about was the Protectorate Deputy Director, Damian Petrie.

Tex glanced around the office until he spotted a holo player. He moved over and inserted the disk.

The images that appeared shocked him. These were recorded conversations with Petrie. Tex listened as Petrie, standing just inches tall, but with a very clear voice and image, set up deal after deal to funnel information to the Dower.

Their arrangement must have been going on for more than a year, at least, judging from the number of recordings on this disk. Tex wondered if the Deputy Director knew he was being recorded. Somehow, he doubted it.

Tex slammed off the holo player and yanked out the disk. He didn't want or need to know any more. He was not in a position to do anything with this information. Worse, he wasn't political enough to know whom to trust and whom *not to* trust. Commander Seton, their controller, worked for the Deputy Director a great deal, so even Seton couldn't be trusted.

Tex knew, standing there in that basement, that no one he knew could be trusted with this.

He put the disk back in the secret file and slammed the door on the disgusting material.

Then he moved to the door and, with a perfect toss, rolled an incendiary grenade under the table with the hidden file, pulled the door closed, and stepped down the hall.

The explosion brought sand and dust down into the hallway and shook everything.

"You all right?" the pilot asked over the comm link.

"Just cleaning up a little business," Tex said. "Almost loaded."

"Ready when you are," the pilot said.

It took Tex only a minute to set the time-delay charge and plant it in the armory.

They had lifted off and were at a safe distance when the remains of the Dower dome exploded from the ground in a cloud of flames and sand and smoke.

The Dower ships were gone, as were the Dower base and most of their agents. But the price for the success had been high. Two outstanding, experienced operatives were lost—*unrecoverable* was the common term—and would never live on in successor clones.

And Tex had information inside his head he had no idea what to do with.

Nor did he know if he should do anything at all.

Chapter Five

Only a few members of the Quorum, high-ranking Protectorate officials, and some intelligence agents know operatives exist. Even fewer know the extent of what they do.

—Mercatante Jones,
Controller

The black-and-gray spaceship lowered itself toward the landing area in the center of the vast cavern. Overhead, the cover moved slowly closed, locking the ship and its roaring engine sound inside. Anyone outside happening to see the ship disappear would think the rock mountain had swallowed it.

Jefferson sat in his formfitting desk chair, watching the ship pass the level of his office. He could feel the vibration of its engines through the stone under his carpet, and he could hear the distant roar through the thick glass. But by and large the ship looked like it was simply floating downward, slowly fitting into a berth below.

Spaceships landing in the cave docking area that lay beyond his window had become commonplace, but this ship was new, the tenth added to their growing fleet. From the reports he had received, it had belonged to the secret police of a Confed planet named Caracol. His people had managed to get inside it and get away with the ship while the forces it had carried were occupied elsewhere. They had bought the pilot's service, but there was no doubt he was already dead.

Or if he wasn't, he would be soon.

The area in which the ship had landed was the largest cavern in this massive complex. The entire place held enough people to be called a small city, with all that entailed, including schools and elderly care. The name of the underground city was Kenyon.

At last measurement it had over a hundred miles of tunnels, many of them large natural caverns, and rooms like his office that had been carved out of the stone. It was dug deep into a mountain range near the equator of a planet called New Bisson.

New Bisson was a half water and half mountainous planet capable of sustaining human colonies only near the equator on the four large islands. Its local planetary government hoped to someday join the Confederation, but it would never get the chance if Jefferson had anything to say about it.

He mostly ignored the locals, bothering with them only when it was easier to ask for something than cause the trouble of just taking it. He had about a third of the politicians on the planet in his pocket, and the other two thirds feared him. None of them knew of this secret underground complex.

In fact, even with more than ten thousand occupants, Kenyon was little more than a rumor on New Bisson and completely unheard of off planet.

His intercom button beeped softly.

"Yes," he said.

"Mr. Jefferson," his secretary said, "a private call from Deputy Director Petrie."

"Through my encrypted line," Jefferson said.

Outside his window, the new ship's engines shut down, cutting off the distant thunder and slight vibration. On the shelf filled with books and memorabilia from his travels sat a tall, alien statue. It was heavy, almost solid gold, and looked like some tall, half-insect–half-bird creature. Very alien in design. It had been a gift from Deputy Director Petrie, and had arrived two days ago.

As far as Jefferson knew, Director Petrie was the only person serving in the higher ranks of the Protectorate who knew of Kenyon. Petrie had helped Jefferson a number of times over the years and been paid richly for the help.

"Chancellor," Petrie said as the image on his vid screen cleared. Chancellor was a title Jefferson held here in Kenyon. Three chancellors ran the place and made all the policy decisions. However, the other two did as Jefferson instructed.

"Director," Jefferson said, putting on his best

smile for a man who might shortly become one of the most powerful individuals in all the Known Worlds. "Thank you for the gift. It's stunning. I have it here in my office."

"You are more than welcome, Chancellor," Petrie said. "It's a Seer religious artifact. I recently came into possession of twelve of them."

Jefferson glanced at the gold statue on his shelf, then back at the screen, the smile on his face turning to amazement as he realized what the statue was. "You're telling me that this is one of the stolen Shadoon statues?"

Petrie laughed. "Nice, isn't it?"

"Very," Jefferson said, laughing along with him. "Very."

"I thought you'd appreciate it," Petrie said.

"So besides allowing me to thank you for such a special gift," Jefferson said, smiling, "what business do you have for me this time around?"

The relationship between Jefferson and Petrie had become one of mutual self-interest. Petrie needed something taken or done; Jefferson and his people would do it in exchange for information and a part of the profit. It was an arrangement known only to the two of them, but it had worked very well so far for both parties.

"No business this time," Director Petrie said, still smiling because his gift had been so well received. "Just a heads-up call."

"On what?" Jefferson asked. This was a first.

"I have information," Petrie said, "that would lead me to believe the Shadoon will be staging an expedition to the Caltair system over the next few days."

Jefferson nodded. The Caltair system was near Kenyon and the New Bisson system. But it was of little significance: three mostly dead planets, one struggling human colony on the second planet, and nothing of any note on the third planet besides an abandoned archaeological site. "Are Confed ships going to be there, watching?" Jefferson asked.

"No," Petrie said, staring directly at the monitor with an expression that said "Don't ask any more."

"Oh, well, in that case," Jefferson said, nodding, "it sounds as if they won't be running into anyone at all. My ships just happen to have assignments away from that system over the next week, as well."

"Better to be safe and make it two," Petrie said, smiling with a look that didn't reach his eyes.

"At least," Jefferson said. "And thanks again for the gift. It will hold a place of honor on my shelf."

"My pleasure," Director Petrie said.

There was a slight pause; then Deputy Director Petrie went on. "Oh, and one more thing. There's a rumor of a pending attack on your fair city."

"An attack?" Jefferson asked, leaning forward.

He was genuinely shocked. He had heard nothing about an attack. "From whom?"

"Not sure of that," Petrie said, "or if the rumor has any basis in fact. Something concerning a revenge issue, but that's all I know. Just wanted to give you a chance to double up your defenses."

"Much appreciated, as always," Jefferson said, without pushing the Director any more. "I will make the information worth your while down the road."

"I know you will," Petrie said, smiling. "Which is why I like doing business with you. And want to continue to do so."

"As would I, Director," Jefferson said.

Petrie just nodded and cut the connection.

Jefferson remained sitting, staring at the screen for a moment, before standing and moving over to pick up the heavy gold statue of the alien.

A Seer sacred statue, treasured beyond all measure by the Sword of Shadoon. Only twelve existed, and last time Jefferson had heard, a Dower ship had taken them from a secret transport headed for Shadoon. Did Petrie understand the power he had just handed Jefferson?

More than likely the Deputy Director understood exactly what he had done.

Jefferson sat the statue down and scooted it away from the edge of the shelf, toward the safety of the back. It wouldn't do to have such a valuable thing fall and be damaged. At least, not until he could use it for all it was worth.

He moved over and tapped his intercom. "Bring me all the ships' schedules for the next two weeks."

"Yes, sir," his secretary said.

He glanced once more at the figure. Better to make sure firsthand that none of his ships got near the system Petrie had marked as off-limits.

He tapped the intercom again. "And set up a meeting with the heads of Kenyon security. One hour."

"Yes, sir," she said again.

When it came to Director Petrie, it was always better to be safe than sorry. Sorry often meant death. And when it came to a direct warning as Petrie had just issued, Jefferson would take no chances. No attack was getting in.

Anyone who tried would die quickly.

Deputy Director Petrie cut the connection to Chancellor Jefferson and sat back, smiling. Jefferson had said he would make the information worthwhile, but what Jefferson didn't know was that he would already be doing Petrie a favor.

Petrie liked playing both ends against the middle, and he hated loose cannons of any type. Jefferson was a loose cannon, but, for the moment, a valuable one.

Petrie swung around and looked out at the

beauty of Wren. The city covered the cliffs and valley floor, flowing architecture surrounded by hundreds of colors of flowers, rock formations, and even a number of waterfalls. His office over-looked paradise, and at times he used that beauty to calm himself and organize his thoughts.

Petrie picked up the file brought to him from Blossom by the two surviving operatives from that mission and glanced through it one more time. The file showed that the Shadoon had been funding various aspects of the NRM movement against the Confed-sanctioned government of Blossom. That was a piece of information that Petrie had not had before. And it wasn't one he was happy about at all.

Since the mission had been successful against the NRM, he wasn't worried about the Shadoon influence there at the moment. But he was deeply concerned about the two operatives' learning that the influence of the Shadoon was spreading. They had found the file and recognized it for its importance. And while operatives were usually smart enough not to talk, the risk remained.

That kind of talk might just get in the way of some of his plans. He couldn't allow that.

Since the controller they had given it to was al-ready one of his people, that was covered. The op-eratives had been taking care of the NRM as a favor Petrie had offered to the leader of Blossom, so if any of the dangerous information leaked at that end, he would be able to control it.

Thus, the only loose ends from the Blossom mission were the operatives who went by the code names Flint and Hawk.

Petrie flipped the file back onto his desk and went back to staring out at the city as the sunlight of the morning worked its way up the cliff face, brightening the colors, glistening off a waterfall.

There was another loose end that bothered him, from yet another mission, and that was the operative known as Tex. He was the only surviving member of the team that had found the Shadoon statues and brought them back, along with a large amount of cash. The cash had been split as it normally would be split, between the operative, the pilot, the controller, and with the appropriate percentage finding its way up and into his hands. Some he would keep, but a large part was channeled to fund more missions.

The statues now sat in a box in his office—or at least nine of them did. Three he had given away, to be used for political leverage later. Something with the value of a Shadoon religious statue made for a powerful bargaining chip. And he still had nine such chips left.

Plus one loose end. Tex.

The pilot was already dead, lost in a tragic accident just two days after returning from the mission. That had been laughably easy to arrange.

But operatives were much harder to deal with. Tex had vanished back into the worlds of the Confed, as all operatives did after a mission, going back to one of perhaps several everyday identities he was likely to maintain, waiting to be called up for another mission.

Petrie knew Tex's real name, where he lived, and just about everything about him since he had joined the service. But attacking him at home wasn't the way to deal with that problem. If the attack failed, Tex might go underground. An angry operative could be a very dangerous enemy.

Still, Petrie hated having that loose end just floating out there.

The answer was simple, really. It had come to him over dinner last night. Tex, Flint, and Hawk would have a new mission to do this very next week. A mission they wouldn't come back from, but their memory chips would survive. No point in wasting good people who were well trained by the Confed, especially when the agents themselves paid to be cloned. Once they were dead, they would be in no position to notice, or protest, any modifications that might be made to the contents of their chips.

Modifications in memories that he would see to personally, to make sure they were done correctly.

Tex would not remember what he had found on his last mission, and Hawk and Flint would have no memory of that orange smell, or of a special file. Once again, they would be valuable resources for the Confed instead of loose ends.

A resource was a resource, after all. Petrie wouldn't have risen this far in the Protectorate if he didn't know how to use resources to his best advantage.

Chapter Six

We have lives that we lead between missions. They might be lonely, might be fractured and often interrupted, but they're the other thing we live for. If you've been cloned a few times, your life is really several people's lives put together. No surprise that few marriages can survive that.

—Snap,

From *Expose*,

an underground journal investigating Operations activities

Tex woke to the sound of faint beeping.

At first he thought he was having another nightmare, being burned again, and the beeping was the timer going off, saying he was well done after being thrown onto his back on a red-hot grill. In the first dreams it was an alien who pressed a fork into him to test Tex's toughness.

The last two times the nightmare had changed. It had been Deputy Director Petrie wielding the fork. It had been better with the alien. At least then the nightmare ended when he awoke.

Tex's burns were healed, but the memory still held on. And the thoughts about what he had found in that hidden desk drawer haunted him like a blip on the radar that he couldn't shake. He had told no one, but it bothered him more than he wanted to admit.

What had Deputy Director Petrie been doing with the Dower? And with the Shadoon? Try as he might, Tex couldn't come up with an answer that benefited Confed security. More than likely it was Petrie using his position to extort money from potential targets and climb to the directorship of the sector. And Petrie didn't seem concerned with how many were killed in the process.

It was the only logical conclusion Tex could come to. The problem was, there was nothing he could do about it. And no one he dared talk to.

Tex rolled over and tried to get back to sleep, pushing the nightmare and the thoughts of Petrie out of his head. But the beeping continued.

"What—?"

He rolled back, trying to force himself to wake up. Then he realized what was happening.

He reached out, and without even turning on the reading light, flicked open the drawer to the nightstand.

The call light was blinking.

"Damn," he said, falling backwards and staring at the ceiling.

Operatives were given the call lights and beepers with a specific frequency, and they were told to place them in their homes. Then, when a call to a mission was sent out, it was in the form of a wide-band encoded broadcast. That way the operative's privacy could be maintained, yet a message could be sent instructing the operative to report to his controller.

The beeping continued.

Tex sat up and stared at the blinking light in his nightstand just to make sure. Then he pounded his fist on the wood and lay back in the dark, disgusted. He could have used a few more weeks of rest. The burns had been hard on him, and it had taken him time to recover. Just yesterday was the first day he had actually felt like himself again.

Outside his home the quiet neighborhood hadn't started to awake yet. There weren't even any traffic sounds from the distant highway.

Just him and the beeping that called him to another mission.

He lay there, staring at the ceiling, remembering the file and Director Petrie's name while at the same time trying to shove the thoughts about the file away.

Finally the beeping stopped.

If he didn't hit the respond button, it would start up again in five minutes. Even though he believed in the importance of his work, there were times he just didn't want to head out on a mission. This was one of those times.

He lay in the silence, staring at the ceiling, thinking back over how he had managed to get to this position. Coming out of school, all he could

think about was joining up, helping the Protectorate. He had gone through basic training without a hitch, and then spent four years climbing
the ranks in the army. During that time he had
gotten to see some pretty strange planets, but hadn't
done anything he thought really important.

So when he had heard through the grapevine
about a special forces group, he had gone to his
CO and volunteered.

At first he had been trained for army special operations; then two days before that training was
to end, he had been offered a chance to really
serve the Confederation. He wasn't told in what
way, but he was told that he had shown he was
qualified for a very special group, if he was interested in laying down his life for the Confed.

He had said yes and been sworn to secrecy. He
had background checks done on him and all his
friends and remaining family. Only then was he
taken to training.

There, a man code-named Vic had been his
trainer. Vic was short, wiry, and he had a long
nose that made him look like a greyhound. From
Tex's point of view, Vic had taken an immediate
dislike to him, shoving him harder than he shoved
any of the others.

Then, about halfway through the training, Vic
started calling him Tex. It had been meant as a
slur, to let people know that Tex was a big, dumb,

lumbering kind of guy. Tex hated it, but the name had stuck.

When he thought about it after all these years, he still hated the name, but he had gotten used to it.

The beeper in the drawer went off again. Outside, a dog barking and the distant noise of a truck cut the stillness.

Duty called.

He reached inside the drawer and punched the respond button, sending a signal to his controller that he had gotten the call. He now had two hours in which to report.

He glanced at the clock on the nightstand, crawled out of bed, and then headed for the bathroom. Maybe by the time this mission was over, he'd know what to do about that file, if anything. More than likely, he would do nothing, and someday the information would die with him.

Maybe even on this mission.

And maybe for the overall health of the Confederation, that was the best thing that could happen.

Hawk flipped her small bag of personal belongings and change of clothes onto a chair in Commander Seton's empty office; then she lowered her bag of weapons and armor slowly to the floor. There were enough explosives in that bag to blow a good-size hole in this building. Missions were dangerous enough. No point in getting careless and killing herself before anything even got started.

"Together again," a voice said from behind her as the office door opened.

Hawk glanced around to see Flint.

Hawk smiled. "Always glad to have you with me on a mission. Always."

"And you with me," Flint said, nodding in return as she lowered her weapons and armor bag to the floor beside a chair.

"Wonder where the Commander has gotten to?" Hawk said, pointing at the empty desk as she dropped into a chair.

Flint just shrugged and sat down, as well.

"More than likely too early for him," Hawk said.

At that moment the door opened and a very large man with an even larger bag of weapons entered. He had short dark hair and a square jaw that gave him the appearance of a moving block.

But something about this man told Hawk that he was much more than just a block with a machine gun. His eyes told her there were brains in that bulk, and the catlike way he moved told her he could do much more than just stomp around.

"Too early for whom?" the man asked, smiling, as he sat his bag on the floor.

"Our controller," Hawk said. She stood and stuck out her hand. "Hawk."

"Tex," the man said. His grasp covered her entire hand and was firm but not crushing.

"Flint," Hawk said, indicating the synthetic she had spent so many missions with.

Flint shook his hand, nodding.

"Your reputation precedes you," Hawk said. She had heard of Tex a number of times since joining operations. He was earning quite the reputation, almost as much as Flint. She might learn something on this mission, whatever it was going to be.

"As does yours," Tex said.

Hawk doubted she had much of a reputation, but it was nice of him to include her. Always better to have a team get off on a good footing. She had argued with team members before, and it just didn't instill the trust she felt was needed to keep them all alive in a tight spot.

The door opened, and Commander Seton, their controller, came in, followed by another man she didn't recognize. He, too, carried a weapons bag, so she assumed he was a fourth member of the team.

Seton was a short man who walked quickly, talked quickly, and couldn't be trusted to walk across the hall without trying to screw someone. Yet he had managed, on some of the toughest missions, to put top teams together and get the job done. In all the infighting between controllers, Hawk had heard Seton was nasty, but he had excellent connections in Operations Division headquarters, and in the Protectorate board itself.

"Earhart," Seton said, indicating the man who had come in with him, "Tex. Flint. Hawk."

Seton pointed to each in turn, and each in turn shook Earhart's hand.

Earhart had blond hair, blue eyes, and a medium build that was clearly strong and quick. Hawk didn't like the look in Earhart's eyes right from the start. It wasn't a look she could trust. As she shook his hand it felt more like Earhart was undressing her with his eyes.

"Okay," Seton said, "we got a tough one facing us. Let's get to it. Gather around."

He spread a map on his desk and pointed to it.

"Kenyon," Seton said, "an underground and very secretive city of almost ten thousand people."

The map was a multilayered maze of tunnels and caverns, and from the scale shown on the map, the place looked huge. Hawk didn't like the looks of that at all.

"The place has a spaceport that can hold up to twenty ships, major public areas, and living sections divided into various neighborhoods."

With each description, Seton pointed to an area of the map, jabbing it with his finger.

"It's guarded like a major military base, only tighter, and it's located in the middle of nowhere, on a planet called New Bisson. New Bisson has human colonies, but it is not a Confed planet as of yet."

"So what's the objective?" Flint asked, getting right to the point.

Seton smiled at her. "Kenyon is a smuggler's haven, ruled like a dictatorship by a three-person council. They control over eighty percent of the illegal drug and contraband trafficking in this region of the Confed, and they've begun trafficking in weapons and other, more destructive devices. The Protectorate wants it cut back."

"So what's the objective?" Flint repeated. "And what's in it for us?"

Hawk smiled as Seton shook his head. She really liked Flint's style.

"Fame, glory, and money," Seton said, "without the fame and glory. And, of course, the gratitude of the Confed."

None of the operatives smiled at that old joke.

Seton went on. "As for what's the target, it's not a what, but a who. This guy."

Seton tossed a photo of a man with a gray mustache wearing an expensive business suit and loud tie. "Chancellor Jefferson. He's one of the three in charge of the place, and he does most of the running of everything."

"The big boss," Earhart said.

"You got it," Seton said. "You can do as much or as little damage as you want on the way in and out. I don't care. Just take out Jefferson."

Hawk stared at the others, then at the map of tunnels and caverns. It looked like a bad op to her, and from the looks on the other operatives' faces, they felt the same way.

Chapter Seven

Operatives go in on a target "clean"—no ID or insignia, no traceable point of origin. They do the op, avoid or eliminate any witnesses, and leave as "clean" as they came. They are the perfect secret weapons.
            —Damian Petrie,
           Deputy Director of Operations, Region Six,
           Introduction to the Controllers' Guide

Tex had never seen such preparation for a mission. He and the other three operatives had gone over the maps of the underground city called Kenyon for five full days, making sure they knew every inch of the place. Commander Seton had pictures of the hallways, the landing bay, the large parklike cavern, and the housing units. He even had pictures of the executive area where the chancellors worked and lived.

But even after days of briefings, this still felt like an absurd mission, and Tex didn't much like that feeling at all. All his missions had looked hard at the start, but none of them had looked so unlikely to succeed.

Tex soaked up everything he could. He knew that sometimes the smallest details made the difference between life and death. Like that low ridge that had separated the Dower spaceships from the dome on his last mission. If he had gone ten more paces over that ridge, he would have died that day. But he had stopped just short of the top, for some reason, which allowed him barely enough time to get out of the way of the blast. Small details make the difference on every mission.

He was relieved to discover that the other operatives on this mission seemed as concerned about the small things, as well. Hawk and Flint seemed to be on top of everything, sometimes asking questions he was about to ask. He had a good feeling about them from the first hand-shake, and as the two days of training went by, he had grown to respect them both.

Earhart, their fourth operative, was another matter. The longer Tex was around him, the less Tex liked him. And he wasn't sure why. The guy talked very little, but Tex wasn't known for his long speeches either.

The guy seemed to be paying attention to the planning and details, but at times Tex wasn't sure Earhart cared. And having an operative on a mission who didn't care if he lived or died wasn't going to be healthy for any of them.

As the briefing went on, Tex found himself with Flint and Hawk more and more.

"Okay," Seton said, tossing both Flint and Hawk a small scanner. "Those things are tuned into a bug we have planted in the head of the Kenyon cartel's main office."

"You got a bug in there?" Hawk asked. "I'm impressed."

Tex was, as well. From what they had been learning about the Kenyon and its operations, it was a closed organization, with tightly regulated traffic and no real contact with the outside, besides maintenance of essential supply channels. Getting a bug in there had to have been a piece of work.

"Take a look at this," Seton said.

He keyed up a large wall screen showing a three dimensional cross section of the Kenyon caves, caverns, and tunnels. Tex had already spent a lot of time poring over that image, comparing it to the maps, making sure he knew the place exactly.

But now on this image, something else had been added. A small green light was blinking regularly in the main office of Chancellor Jefferson.

"We're getting that feed directly from a satellite in orbit around New Bisson," Seton said. Then he pointed to the two small scanners Flint and Hawk were holding. "When you're in the caves, those scanners are set to key in on that bug. It will help you get to your objective in case you get lost."

"Nice touch," Hawk said. "But I have one big question: How are we going to get inside that mountain to use these things?"

Tex had been wondering about that one big detail right from the start.

Seton had showed them pictures and topographical maps of the mountains Kenyon occupied. There were no roads leading into or out of the area. Not even a trail. And the mountains, besides being rough and steep, were well guarded and booby-trapped almost beyond reason.

Everything went in by spaceship, dropping down through what was a blind corridor in the New Bisson planetary radar system. All food, weapons, and supplies. Everything, hauled in there from other planets. Nothing was bought locally on New Bisson.

Finally, just when Tex figured he had to ask, Hawk had brought the subject up.

"Crossed my mind, as well," Tex said. "Not only in, but let's not forget out."

Flint nodded, but Earhart acted as if he already knew. If he didn't, that attitude bothered Tex. But if Earhart already knew, that might imply another, completely different problem.

Seton only laughed. "We thought about Farcasting you in, but that's too experimental at this point. Instead, there's a daily transport ship that goes from a nearby Confed world called Zona Three. The Kenyons have a large supply base there, which takes all kinds of food and equipment shipments from a dozen different worlds and then routes them into Kenyon once a day."

"And that base isn't guarded?" Hawk asked before Tex could.

"Oh, it's heavily guarded," Seton said. "And the transport ship has an armed escort in flight between Zona Three and Kenyon on New Bisson."

"So where's the hole in the system?" Tex asked. "I'll wager the goods are scanned and searched coming into Zona Three, so we can't sneak in hidin' in some crate."

"Exactly," Hawk said, nodding. "And the ship is defended en route, so there's no taking it along the way without alerting the Kenyon base ahead."

Tex agreed with that statement. "I don't see the opening to insert us in that mountain."

Seton pointed them toward a wall screen and punched a button on his desk. The image of the caves and the blinking bug light vanished as he brought up an image of the entire planet known as New Bisson, a water-covered world with more islands than anyone could count. Kenyon was inside a large mountain range on the sixth biggest island.

On the image, the nonradar corridor through which the Kenyon ships came down appeared as a funnel, tight on the surface, wide at the top.

"Our opening is here," Seton said, pointing to a place at the top of that corridor. "As the cargo ship enters low orbit, the escort ship breaks away and heads back. Sensors on the cargo ship are blurred during atmosphere entry."

"So we're in a shielded shuttle, holding a position in low orbit," Tex said. "Waitin' to tag along with the cargo ship. Right?"

"Exactly," Seton said. "You'll follow them down that corridor like a shadow."

"What about the ground radar in Kenyon?" Flint asked.

Commander Seton smiled. "I have arranged for a small shuttle from one of the regular colonies on New Bisson to be in orbit near where you will be waiting. As the cargo ship passes, the unmanned shuttle will send out a distress call and request emergency landing."

"A decoy," Hawk said.

Tex nodded, impressed at the plan as Commander Seton went on. "The unmanned shuttle comes in on a trajectory close behind the cargo ship, explodes early in reentry, and the signature and reentry burn of your team's shuttle is explained by the debris."

Hawk and Flint were both nodding, staring at the image.

Even Tex had to admit, the plan might work. Then he got the surprise he wasn't expecting.

"Earhart will be piloting the team's ship," Seton said.

"What?" Hawk asked, glancing first at Earhart, then at Seton, the look on her face telling Tex she wasn't happy with that news. Earhart had been in on this entire mission before them.

Commander Seton laughed. "Think about it. It's perfect."

"I have thought about it, and I don't like it," Hawk said. "A complicated stunt like this demands a professional pilot."

Tex had to agree, but he didn't get a chance to say anything before Seton went on.

"Since there's no way a shuttle could get in there," Seton said, "drop a team, and get back out that roof door quickly enough to make it in one piece, we decided to have the shuttle land and be parked there, waiting for you to complete your mission. That meant that the pilot had to be an operative."

"I used to pilot in the Navy," Earhart said, smiling at Hawk's angry frown. "Before I joined Operations. Trust me, I can get us all safely into and out of that place."

"So that ship's our exit, as well?" Tex asked.

"That, or any other ship sitting on the ground, available for you to commandeer, if necessary," Seton said.

"I can fly almost anything," Earhart said, his voice level. It was clear to Tex that he wasn't trying to brag. It was just a fact to him.

"I'm going to leave the shuttle's engines running on standby," Earhart said. "Thumbprint-protect the controls. No one but me can turn them off."

"Quick getaway," Tex said, slowly starting to warm to the idea.

"And the nice trick," Seton said, "is that if you four don't return in two hours, the shuttle's core overloads and blows."

"Which shuts down the Kenyon operation pretty quickly," Tex said, "even if we can't."

"So we fly in on a bomb," Hawk said, "do the job, and with any luck get out on the same bomb before it explodes. Wonderful." She was shaking her head, clearly disgusted at the idea.

Tex flashed back to the explosion at Dower. He couldn't imagine that kind of explosion inside a network of caves and tunnels. No one would survive it. And this time there were ten thousand people in the way in those caves. He didn't like that backup plan at all.

"Exactly," Seton said, smiling, ignoring Hawk. "You go after the head, and if that fails, we blow up the body. If you can't make it out on your own, you should still have time to exit the facility and move to a safe distance. You'll have a beacon transmitter with you; after the town blows, turn it on and wait for pickup—if I don't see you back here in four hours, we'll be looking for you."

"It better not come to that," Flint said.

Tex could only agree.

"How much longer are we going to double the guards around the mountain?" Arington asked.

"We're spending a lot of time and manpower on this vague tip you got."

Jefferson stared at the Kenyon chief of security standing in front of his desk. The guy was short, with chopped black hair that stood on end and muscles on top of muscles. He wore a tight T-shirt, and a pistol rode on his hip.

"We keep it for as long as I say we keep it." There was no way Jefferson was going to tell Arington just where the tip had come from, and why he was acting on it. His relationship with Director Petrie was his own business, and he didn't plan on telling anyone about it now.

"Oh, I know that," Arington said without backing down. Arington was as mean as they came, and Confed-trained in a dozen different ways of war. He was the one who had designed all the unique safeguards of the Kenyon defense system, and so far, in five years, there had been no breaches. Jefferson trusted him as much as he trusted anyone.

"So what's the problem?" Jefferson asked.

"Exactly what I said," Arington replied. "I'm just wondering how long using the extra guards is going to be? More than another week, and I've got to start training some new men right now."

Jefferson nodded. "Start training. The tip is credible, and until I'm given the all clear, we keep up the extra guards' shifts."

Arington nodded. "I'm going to need to pull

men from the cargo area, as well as maintenance and construction."

"Take what you need, but *only* what you need," Jefferson said.

"Understood, sir," Arington said. With that he turned and left, closing the door behind him, leaving Jefferson alone in his office.

The gold Seer statue sat on the shelf, mocking him. He wished he could just call Director Petrie and ask him where he got the tip, and find out if he had any further information. But he knew he couldn't. The Director had been kind enough to tell him of the threat in the first place, for some reason Jefferson did not yet know. The least Jefferson could do was make sure he acted on the tip. And if it turned out to be accurate, he would owe the Director more than he already did.

A distant clanking sound echoed through his office, and Jefferson swung his chair around to look out over the huge cavern that was the docking bay. Above the space, the giant door was sliding back out of the way, allowing a ship to enter. Watching the occasional ship come and go was one of his few pleasures.

Jefferson glanced at his watch. The cargo ship was right on time.

Suddenly the comm link on his desk beeped.

He turned and hit the button. "Yes?"

"Sir, a New Wren colony shuttle is having trouble right over us, in low orbit, and it's asking the New Wren colony controllers for permission to make an emergency landing on the island."

"Track the ship with the AA cannons," Jefferson ordered. "If it gets too close to our supply ship, or the cargo doors, blow it out of the sky. And if it does land, get a team on it right away."

"Understood, sir."

As the docking bay door got just over halfway open, Jefferson could see through the portal, the cargo ship slowing for a controlled entry. The ship would time its passage through the top of the hill at just the moment the big sliding door reached its full width, and by the time it landed and cut its engines, the door would be almost closed again.

It was a system of timing that Arington had insisted upon. He had pointed out that the base's defenses were at their most vunerable at the moment that door was open.

That worry had lead to the development of the timed openings of the major cargo bay door, and the radar scans of the approach to Kenyon.

Suddenly, high in the sky over the dome, something exploded in a blinding flash of white. Through the open cargo bay doors Jefferson saw burning debris shoot out in all directions.

The comm link beeped again.

"What was that?" Jefferson asked into the comm.

"Sir, the intruder ship simply blew up."

"Understood," Jefferson said.

One problem solved almost as quickly as it had happened. He wished most of the problems he faced were that easy.

He turned and watched as the big doors clanged fully open, accepting the massive cargo ship. Above the cargo ship the debris was still falling from the explosion. Luckily it was slightly to one side, and nothing was coming at the big cargo bay and the ship.

The big ship entered the mountain, easing downward as it did every day, settling toward the main loading berth.

Then suddenly the intruder alert sounded, its siren echoing through the caves and tunnels. In all the years, he had heard those sirens only on training exercises. And since he had not ordered an exercise, this had to be for real.

Red lights began blinking all over the massive landing bay, and above the bay the big doors had already begun to close. The big cargo ship kept moving slowly downward, the middle of it passing his window now. He was just about to punch his comm button and ask Arington what was happening, when he saw the reason for himself.

A small black shuttle, small enough to fit easily inside the cargo ship, was coming in very fast, right behind the bigger ship.

So the other ship's explosion had been nothing more than a decoy, to make sure their radar systems didn't track this intruder. Smart planning.

Someone had gone to a lot of effort to get a ship in here.

As he watched, the small ship made it through the closing cargo bay doors and swung wide. It looked like it was headed toward a side docking port, just under his office. It was a private port he used to land his private ship. A ship that was, at the moment, being refitted ten light-years away.

The black ship, a sleek corporate model, flashed past his window, coming in far faster than any pilot should have dared.

"Sir," Arington said over the comm, "we have an intruder ship that has just landed hard in the private docking area."

"I saw it," Jefferson said. "Take care of it, and make sure you find out who they are before you're done."

"Understood, sir," Arington said. "Are you moving to your safety bunker?"

The safety bunker was a place where the three chancellors were supposed to go during emergencies of this sort. He hated the windowless room with the big steel doors and uncomfortable furniture.

"Staying right here," Jefferson said. "I'll notify you if I feel the need to move. Now find out who's aboard that ship, and keep me posted."

"Yes, sir," Arington said.

Jefferson moved to the window and tried to

look down the cliff face beneath it to the dock below. It wasn't possible, but he tried anyway.

At that moment, the big cargo ship finally touched down, and overhead, the sliding door that sealed in the transport bay rolled closed with a clang.

"Well, whoever it is got in," Jefferson said aloud, staring at all the activity below him as security personnel took up their posts. "Now what are they going to do?"

Chapter Eight

The politics of the Protectorate, especially in its "black budget" agencies like the Operations Division, are not so different from the politics of a petty crime organization. They just take place on a larger scale, and with higher priced goods and services.

—Betsy Randall,
Quorum delegate from Garden Five,
from her autobiography

Tex had himself braced as the small shuttle fired its emergency landing thrusters, bounced hard on the rock landing pad, glanced off one wall of the berth, and came to rest on its pylons.

Whatever his feelings for Earhart, Tex had to admit he was a damn good pilot. He had taken them in and gotten the little four-seater on the ground faster than Tex would have believed possible, especially with the big cargo ship and a lot of rock walls in their way.

"Go! Go! Go!" Hawk shouted as the hatch slammed open onto the rock pad.

Earhart had brought them in so the hatch faced the stone wall, using the ship to block fire from the large cargo bay area. They had only a few seconds to get out and into the positions they had selected beforehand. Tex and Seton had thought the positions were at least defensible, though for how long was another issue. But they didn't have to be there long, if things went well.

The master plan was to get through a large, gray door set in the wall precisely where the ship's hatch had opened, into the small hallway beyond, and then into the large main hallway. From there they would move up to the executive suites, find Jefferson, and toast him.

Tex had no doubt it was going to be a fight every step of the way, both in and out. He had bought new armor just for the mission, and had no doubt it was going to get tested to the max.

Flint was outside and planted against the far rock wall off to the right before the sound of the hatch hitting stone had finished echoing through the wailing alarm sirens that filled the large cavern.

Hawk was one step behind her, going left to a position under a rock ledge to the left of the closed door.

Tex, a minigun out and ready, stepped onto the ramp and stopped, facing the door. There were no markings on it. Just a plain gray door with a silver handle. The door had an electronic lock of some kind, and Hawk immediately went to work on it, setting it up to open on command.

"Ready, Earhart?" Tex asked.

Earhart had the hardest task. He had had to land the ship, set the explosives and timer, get his own weapons, and get into position to back up Tex.

"Go!" Earhart said, emerging from the cockpit area, rifle up and ready. He was sweating and slightly pale, but smiling nonetheless.

Tex liked it when his teammates smiled. It made him feel more confident.

Hawk finished the quick electronic bypass, which was one of her special skills Tex had learned about when they trained for this mission. "There goes the lock," she said.

"Open it!" Tex said, snapping the second mini-gun into his left hand, so now he had two aimed at the door.

Hawk nodded, tapped a button, and stepped back out of the way.

Three guards dressed in green uniforms and carrying pistols were caught by surprise when the door swung open. Before they could react, Tex cut them down with blasts from both guns, their bodies were shredded by solid streams of bullets.

Another guard about halfway down the short hallway was also killed instantly, his blood spraying over the stone wall as he did a somersault and landed square on his back.

"Clear," Tex said, stopping his fire. He put one

gun back on his shoulder, but kept the other aimed down the corridor that now opened up in front of him. From the maps they had studied for so long, Tex knew this short corridor opened up into a very wide and long main corridor.

From that main tunnel came the sounds of screaming as regular base personnel ran for cover, some stupidly running past the end of the hallway in front of Tex. The alarm warnings were still blaring, and combined with the people screaming, the sound inside the caverns was almost painful.

The ceiling of this side corridor wasn't much higher than Tex's head, and the corridor's length was only about twenty paces. But if their Intel was accurate, the main corridor ahead had high ceilings, sometimes up to twenty meters tall, and in places was wide enough for parks with trees to grow in the center without getting in the way of traffic.

The residents of this place called that big corridor Parkway, and it ran for hundreds of meters, slowly slanting downward to the right from their location, and up to the left, serving as one of the main arteries for the entire city.

Hawk went down the small corridor ahead of Tex, staying along the wall, pistol in one hand, organic detector in the other, making sure she wasn't going to be surprised by anyone coming around the corner in front of her.

She made the main corridor without firing a shot, looked quickly in both directions, like a kid crossing a busy street, and then ducked to the left.

"Clear," she said a moment later.

Tex could see from his position that the last of the civilians had finally disappeared from the Parkway, fleeing down side corridors away from them. Smart people.

Flint and Earhart went onto Parkway next, both at full run, rifles pointed ahead. Flint went right.

Tex watched as Earhart made it, in about ten running strides, to a park bench on some grass in the middle of the corridor.

No one shot at them; no one tried to stop them. It seemed that coming into that one small landing platform, so far above the rest of the docking area, had caught everyone off guard, as it had been intended to do.

Tex glanced behind, down the narrow hall they had just exited. The ship was serving as a perfect shield for them, blocking what they were doing from view of the big cargo bay, and all the guards above and below the ship. To make that work, Earhart had had to park the ship damn close to the rock wall.

He had done just that. An amazing piece of flying.

Tex stood in the hallway, waiting. He hated

waiting once a battle started. His natural inclination was to just plow ahead and face what there was to face. But that wasn't the plan. He had to wait while Hawk did her job scouting.

Across the open Parkway, Earhart nodded to some hand gesture Hawk must have made, then cut right away from the park bench, and disappeared. Earhart and Hawk both knew exactly where they were heading. They all figured that getting out of this narrow hallway and into the open was the most dangerous part of the start of the mission.

Once out in the wide Parkway corridor, they could hold their own, of that Tex had no doubt.

Behind him the hatch on the ship automatically slammed closed, and he knew the explosive timer had started. Thirty seconds had passed.

That was the time delay they had all agreed on. Thirty seconds from the moment the hatch opened to the moment it slammed closed. Enough time for them to get out, not enough time for anyone else to get inside.

Thirty seconds had seemed short when discussing it in Seton's office. In battle time those thirty seconds had seemed long. Now another timer started. In two hours, the ship's core would explode. If they didn't get back within those two hours and shut it down, these caverns were going to be dealing with the same level of explosion he had barely survived on Dower.

Tex had no plans on trying to ride out a core explosion inside a cave. He was either going to be back here and out of this place in two hours, or he'd die trying.

Rifle shots echoed through the stone tunnels as Flint and Hawk and Earhart picked off the first of the advancing defenders. Tex knew it would take time to move a large security force against them in a place this size, and they didn't plan on letting the Kenyon security have that kind of time.

"Here I come," Tex said. "Ship is locked up and timer set."

He finished reloading his two guns and stepped forward toward the end of the small side hallway. "Ready or not."

"Ready," Hawk said.

"Then we're moving," Tex said.

He moved into the wide hallway and turned left, his minigun pointing forward in his hands. He always felt 100 percent alive in battle situations. Every nerve, every sense on full alert. It was as if a spotlight had been turned on. Every detail sprang into vivid clarity.

Around him the wide corridor smelled of green plants, gunpowder, and blood. The stone ceiling and walls were gray, with some fake, treelike decorations. The thought of all the rock over his head felt like a weight, pressing him down into the stone. How people lived years in a cave complex like this was beyond him. But from all reports, almost ten thousand people lived here.

The alarm sirens suddenly shut off, leaving the place feeling more like a tomb.

His steps were the only sounds breaking the silence.

"Now that's creepy," Hawk said from her position against the left wall, in an alcove.

"I hate silence," Flint said. She was moving to a new position ahead of Tex along the right wall. Earhart was somewhere behind him, guarding their flank.

"Why'd they turn those off?" Hawk asked.

"Maybe they forgot we were here," Earhart said.

"Maybe they couldn't hear themselves think," Flint said.

Tex said nothing. He just kept walking, gun aimed forward, watching every detail. Living here, so far underground, made no sense to him. He liked the open spaces and the feel of the wind on his face. There wasn't much wind in a tunnel. And very little open space.

He strode up the wide, plant-filled hallway like he owned the place, his boots clicking on the rock floor. At the moment he did own the place, and would until they could take it away from him. He liked that feeling, he had to admit.

To the left Hawk continued moving along the wall, gliding smoothly and silently as any good scout could do, finding cover and pausing, then moving forward, matching Tex's steady speed. It took some of the edge off, knowing she was the trailblazer.

Behind him Earhart selectively picked off someone who had dared poke a head out into the open. His two shots were sudden, echoing blasts that broke the stillness.

"Problem?" Hawk asked, not bothering to look back.

"Not anymore," Earhart answered.

"Roger that," Tex said.

About a hundred paces in front of him five security men in the matching green uniforms made the mistake of not looking where they were going when they burst from a side corridor and into the openness of Parkway.

"Oops," Tex said.

Before even Hawk could get off a shot, Tex's gun filled Parkway with a loud roar as he cut the guards apart, leaving the five to tumble head-over-heels into bloody piles of flesh and uniform on a large patch of grass.

"Rushing like that always causes accidents," Hawk said.

"A lot of people make that mistake," Tex said.

Two hundred paces up the large tunnel, two other guards came into sight from a side tunnel. Hawk, in two quick shots, dropped them like rag dolls before they could find cover.

"Nice shootin'," Tex said, his pace smooth and consistent.

"Thanks," Hawk said.

So far, so good.

Tex kept walking, as if he were out for a Sunday stroll.

Flint caught two more far, far up Parkway, out of Tex's range by a long ways, with shots that sent other guards scrambling back to cover.

Two hundred paces from the side corridor that led to their ship, the team arrived at a staircase of grand design, cut out of the rock on the right side of the Parkway, which wound upward to the next level. There was an open feel to the staircase as it curved around the face of the cliff and up to the high-ceilinged cavern of the area above.

"Our target is behind us and up one level," Hawk said, glancing at the scanner trained on the bug someone had planted in Jefferson's office.

It was amazing to Tex that the security in this place hadn't caught the stray signal. Someone had fallen down on the job, and it was going to cost the boss his life.

Getting up the staircase was another issue they had talked about in Seton's office a great deal. They had finally decided it was best to just let Earhart and Flint take up protective positions to guard the big Parkway corridor and then have Hawk take up a position that allowed her to see up the staircase and pick off any resistance with her rifle.

Tex would simply march up the stairs and take a defensible position at the top, holding it long enough to allow the others to advance.

Tex had suggested the idea, and the plan worked just as they had envisioned it in Seton's office.

Hawk cut down three different guards who tried to get into position to take on Tex as he started up the staircase.

Tex, on the climb, didn't have to fire a shot, but in the big, high-ceilinged cavern at the top, he got return fire from eight guards stationed near the mouth of a corridor leading to the executive suites. One of their shots nicked his neck, and he could feel the warmth of the blood flowing down into his armor. He ignored it, yanked his second machine gun off his shoulder, and returned fire.

Three guards, again in the standard green uniform of this place, were hiding behind some planters made of clay and wood. He blew the planters away with a sustained blast, killing the guards behind them.

Three others he caught before they could get to new and better cover, leaving them bleeding or dead in the hallway.

Then with alternating blasts from each of his guns, he held the remaining two guards down in their rock cover.

"Little help up here," Tex said.

"On our way," Hawk said.

A moment later Hawk and Flint joined him and got to different cover as Earhart stopped halfway up to watch the bottom of the staircase.

"Ready?" Tex asked.

Hawk nodded, her rifle aimed at the position of the pinned-down guard on her side of the hall.

Tex stopped shooting, put one gun back over his shoulder, and stepped back.

The two defenders poked their heads out into the open, just as he knew they would, rifles up to return fire.

Fatal mistake.

"Clear," Hawk said.

A moment later Earhart hit the top of the stairs at a run and took up a post in front of a short side corridor.

Tex stepped over one of the bodies and headed down the wide corridor going back in the direction they had just come, his gun up and ready.

From what Tex could tell, they had all suffered a few nicks so far. Earhart had a good scratch along one arm, Hawk was bleeding from one hand, and Flint had a good-size dent in the side of her stomach armor that must have hurt like hell when it took the bullet.

But so far they were all right. Considering that they had just marched up a stone corridor with people shooting at them, the wounds they had sustained were minor.

This executive hallway was the width of a normal house, and the stone floor was carpeted with thick padding. The stone walls were mostly covered with wood paneling, showing stone only wherever there was a decorative planter. There was no doubt he was in the elite-class area. The guys who ran this place forced everyone else to walk on stone while they got plush carpet and wood walls. Figured.

"Heads up!" Earhart said.

Tex stepped into one of the plant alcoves just as a massive firefight broke out behind him.

"They're stuck," Hawk said from a position just behind him and on the other side of the wide hallway.

Tex could see the problem clearly. Flint and Earhart were both pinned down by about ten guards who were timing their shots so perfectly that neither operative could even fire back.

The guards had come in from a side tunnel on the left and had taken excellent positions behind support beams and stone corners. This was the first time the security forces had shown any real intelligence. The guards were going to be tough to dig out of there, and the mission didn't allow them the time to try.

Tex, with one mini still slung over his shoulder,

took out two incendiary grenades. He held one up for Hawk to see.

She nodded. "Good thinking."

He opened up with one of his machine guns blasting away, chasing the attackers back to cover, then walked toward them until he was even with Flint and Earhart's position. Then he tossed the two grenades.

"Cover!" he said, stepping sideways with one more blast from the mini as the two grenades rolled silently along the carpeted floor to a point just behind the attackers' positions.

Tex flattened himself against the wall just inside a doorway as the grenades went off.

He was still a little too close for comfort. The concussion rang his ears, and the heat flash seemed far hotter than he had expected.

"Cooked 'em," Earhart said.

"Well done, I hope," Hawk said, easing back out of her spot, ready to pick off anything that moved. "I think you burned off my eyebrows."

At a glance Tex could tell the two grenades had done the trick. The entire area was burning, smoke billowing from the carpet, planters, wood walls, and bodies. The smoke swirled and then was pulled off down the hallway in the direction away from them. They were lucky the prevailing ventilation in this area moved the air in that direction, otherwise they'd be fighting their way through smoke-choked corridors that smelled of burning flesh. Tex had done that a few times before and was glad he didn't have to do it again now.

"Let's go before the wind shifts," Hawk said.

Tex was already on the move, again strolling down the carpeted hallway; Hawk just a few steps behind him, was moving along the wall, monitoring the directions beeper for the bug and the organic sensor to make sure no one caught them by surprise.

Ahead, two well-dressed women poked their heads out a door, saw them, and screamed. They jumped backwards, slamming the door so hard it echoed down the hall like a shot.

"Civilians," Flint said.

"I hear Tex always gets that reaction from women," Hawk said.

Tex laughed.

The two women definitely hadn't look armed. Operations rules of engagement, while substantially looser than those of other Protectorate forces, and which often featured specific civilians as targets, nevertheless still frowned upon unnecessary casualties. Tex knew that the main rationale for this was that ops should attract as little attention, and leave as small a footprint, as possible. Also, every dead noncombatant was ammunition for those who agitated in the Quorum against the Protectorate.

"Here," Hawk said, pointing at the large wooden door directly ahead.

Tex nodded. Hawk could open the locked door in a very short time, but there didn't seem to be a point with this one. Tex opened fire on the door, and the wood splintered and exploded inward under the intense hail of bullets.

A single-shot pistol returned fire from inside, and a bullet actually grazed him on the hand. A second glanced off his forearm armor and nipped the tip of his left ear.

Tex stepped forward, snapped the second machine gun down into his hand, and then opened up, both guns firing full out.

The fake wooden walls that had been put over the stone exploded. Inside the room, paintings ripped apart, a chair became so much kindling, and shelves flew off the wall.

Firing two minis at full speed inside a rock-walled room pretty much left nothing untouched, including the woman with the pistol crouched behind her desk. She was riddled and very dead by the time Tex stopped his short blasts.

"That door," Hawk said, pointing at the inner door to the left of the big desk.

Tex blew it open.

No return fire came from there.

"There's one body in there," Hawk said. "Directly against the far wall, sitting at a desk in front of a window."

Tex stepped into the doorway, his two machine guns leveled at the man sitting behind the desk. There was no sign of a gun, or any defensive weapon whatsoever. The man's hands were placed flat on the desktop, offering no threat.

From the pictures they had studied, Tex knew at once it was their target, Jefferson.

Tex flipped one gun back up over his shoulder, never letting the other move from aiming at the man's chest.

"You could have just knocked," Jefferson said, smiling and shaking his head. "Those doors were real wood—you know what that cost me?"

Protectorate Regional Deputy Director Petrie strode from the concert hall with the pace of a man who was in a hurry. Not that he was worried about the mission on New Bisson, but actually he was looking forward to the news. For him, the mission was one of those wonderful win-win situations that didn't come up often in life.

If the operatives didn't make it, he would recover their chips and have them cloned, at the operatives' expense, of course. Each clone would have no memory of the files, or statues, or anything that they should not have seen, since these chips could also be scanned and changed, fine-tuning the memories that would be implanted in a full-body clone. It was possible for a clone to have no idea he or she even was a clone.

On this mission, he was looking forward to getting the chips back from three top operatives.

Of course, on the outside chance that the operatives succeeded, then Kenyon and Chancellor Jefferson would no longer be an issue for him to have to deal with.

Win-win. And soon the outcome would be determined.

Around him, the evening seemed perfect. At this time of the year, the warm weather and sun-filled days around Wren made the beautiful city even more enchanting, especially in the evenings when the fresh night air kept the wonderful smells of the different flowers tucked into the canyon.

On nights like this, he loved to walk. The temperature was perfect, the sky full of stars, the cliff faces alive with lights. He planned on going through the park, up the staircase beside the waterfall, and across the skywalk to the area of his office. By then a report on the New Bisson mission might have arrived. If not, he would call the controller and wait for the answer on his balcony, all the while enjoying a snifter of brandy.

"In a hurry, Deputy Director?"

The voice made him stop and turn, his best smile frozen on his face.

Quorum delegate Jane Oxford stood off to one side of the walk. She stepped toward him, not even offering her hand. She was a short woman with bright white hair and a radiant smile that Petrie saw only on public broadcasts. With him she usually reserved a cold, dark-eyed stare that seemed to absorb his self-confidence like a black hole absorbed light. He figured that stare was the reason her husband had died so young. No one could live with that look for long. No one would want to.

Clearly tonight she was dressed for work, not attending a concert, so running into him had not been an accident. She had been waiting.

Oxford represented the planet Barsaan in the Quorum, and she was one of the most powerful people in all the Confederation. Her oversight committee was in charge of the budget for the Protectorate, and she was one of only a few Quorum members who even knew operatives existed, let alone how the Confed used them.

She had no problem with how the operatives did their job. And she was sent reports of every mission. She frequently seemed concerned with why a mission was sent in the first place, from what Petrie could tell by her questions. Since the *why* he needed a mission done often conflicted with the *why* in the report, this made him edgy. Oxford had asked questions a lot lately, and was asking more each week. And along the way, she had made it clear she didn't much like him.

And he didn't like her, as well. In fact, he had more nightmares about her and her self-important oversight committee than about anything else. And now, here she was, ruining a perfectly good win-win night after a fine concert on a beautiful evening.

"I understand there is a mission at the moment, on New Bisson," she said.

He glanced around, not willing to talk about classified operative missions on a public sidewalk. He also used the moment to contain his shock at the fact she knew of the New Bisson mission. Commander Seton, the controller, had said he would make no reports until after the mission had ended. And Petrie had paid him very well for that oversight in normal filing procedures.

Petrie looked her right in the eye. "I would be glad to talk to you about such matters in a secure room. But not here."

"Good," she said, nodding, as if she had hoped that would be his answer. "Follow me."

She turned and started down the sidewalk.

"Mrs. Oxford," Petrie said, standing his ground, "I'm afraid I have other business this evening."

"Cancel it, Deputy Director," she said without glancing over her shoulder.

She knew for a fact he would not dare go against her, especially since she had been clear about the reason for her request. He would have to go along.

He moved to fall into step beside her. Suddenly the wonderful, warm evening after a fine concert didn't seem so win-win.

Chapter Nine

Honestly, the only way you can make sense of the plans of some of these ops is if the destruction of the team is part of the final objective.

—Lew,
conversation overheard
two days before his death

For a moment Tex considered blasting the smile right off of Chancellor Jefferson's face. No man should look that relaxed, that in control, while staring down the barrel of a machine gun. The guy had been lucky enough to not be killed when Tex blasted his door open.

Yet Jefferson did look relaxed and seemed very much in control, as if he were talking to a secretary about a trivial filing problem. Either Jefferson knew far more than Tex did, or he was a superman who couldn't be killed, or he was the best actor in the Known Worlds. Tex was betting on the last option, since the guy was a politician.

"I was told you might be coming," Jefferson said. "I'd offer you folks a chair and a drink, but I doubt you'd accept."

"Told we were coming?" Hawk asked. She had

moved to one side of his desk to see what was in between Jefferson and his desk. She kept her rifle aimed directly at his head. "Who told you?"

Flint and Earhart had taken positions out in the hallway. So far they were finding no resistance coming at them, but Tex knew that for every second they wasted here, getting out became that much harder.

Amazingly, Jefferson laughed. "Deputy Director Petrie, of course. Who else?"

Tex actually jerked at the mention of Petrie. It was like a bad dream suddenly yanked into reality. Tex had seen Petrie's name in a file that connected him with supporting the Dower group, and supplying the Shadoon. Now a deputy director of the Protectorate was warning targets that his own operatives were coming. Why? It made no sense.

"Sure he did," Hawk said, the disgust in her voice clear as a bell. "You're just pulling names out of the air, trying to save your ass."

Jefferson shrugged, still looking calm and collected, even with the two machine guns and one rifle pointed at him. "No way I can prove it to you without you keeping me alive."

"Not likely," Tex said.

"And why would I want proof?" Hawk asked.

Tex glanced at Hawk. She was going for the bait.

"Any good soldier wants proof that there's something rotten on the home front," Jefferson said, staring directly at Hawk. "You're representing the interests of the Confed, risking your lives for the greater good, not for some crook like Petrie whose only goal is to climb the political ladder, all the while getting rich off your blood and toil."

Hawk glanced at Tex; clearly that had her startled.

Tex felt the same way. How did this guy even know they were working for the Confed? Nothing on them, or about their missions could be traced back to any Confed source, including the funding or the ships.

"Garbage," Hawk said. "Who said we were working for the Confed?"

"Only Director Petrie, the man I've been doing business with, would want me dead. Our little city here is gaining too much power for his tastes, and he doesn't like it. So he sent you. Therefore, you must be ops. You're too good to be anything else; otherwise, you never would have pulled off such a clean insertion."

Jefferson shrugged and smiled, his manner as calm as if he were making light conversation over lunch. Why was this man so calm, so certain that he was going to keep on living, that he was just talking?

Suddenly Tex realized the guy was just buying time for something.

Beyond the window, a slight movement on the cliff face opposite Jefferson's window caught Tex's eye. Without moving his head, Tex shifted his gaze out the window.

Snipers were taking positions across the large cavern. In a few seconds he and Hawk would be dead if he didn't move now.

"Hawk! Down!" Tex shouted.

Tex opened up with his machine gun, smearing the top half of Jefferson against the window and smashing the window outward in a thousand pieces of blood-splattered glass.

The sickening smile on the man's face was gone forever. Tex figured he had just done the universe a big favor.

Hawk moved instantly, dropping to the ground as if every muscle in her body had left her.

Tex spun and dived for cover against the front of the large desk as armor-piercing shots cut through the air where he had been standing. Fist-size holes appeared in the wall behind them.

Hawk rolled and came up under the window, out of the line of fire.

One more second of talking with that idiot, and he and Hawk would have been dead, like rank amateurs.

That was the last time he would ever let that happen.

Tex got to his knees, using the front of Jefferson's big wood desk for cover. Between the top, the drawers, and the front panels, the desk was thick enough to slow down just about anything, at least enough that his own armor could handle what made it through.

"We've got a lot of company," Earhart said.

The sound of gunfire from the hallway filled the office, mixing with a consistent barrage of shots from across the large cavern. Bullets pounded into the carpet and walls around Tex, some cutting through the desk.

"Target's been taken out," Tex reported.

"But now what do we do?" Hawk asked. "The bastard slowed us down just enough to let his shooters get into position. He must have one helluva good head of security, for all the good it did him."

She was right. They were pinned down, and from the sounds of it, so were Earhart and Flint. Plus with Jefferson dead, the defenders might just resort to grenades or incendiaries.

They had to get out of this office, and fast.

More shots cut through the room from the now shattered window, smashing into the shelves on the wall, causing books to explode in bursts of paper. The shots made Tex glance at the shelf, just as a golden statue fell to the ground and bounced hard into the middle of the carpet not far from his position.

Tex could not believe what he was seeing. There, on the floor, was one of the twelve Seer statues he had brought back from Dower. The last thing he had known about the statues, Commander Seton had said he had given them to a Protectorate director "to make sure they got into the right hands."

The face on the statue stared at him from the floor with its alien grimace, mocking him.

Tex had been paid for the recovery of the statues, and had thought nothing more of it. But here was one again, right after Jefferson had mentioned Petrie's name.

Commander Seton and Damian Petrie? Tex didn't like how this was adding up.

"Hawk," Tex said, "use the scanner for the bug."

"Why?" Hawk said, easing along the wall under the window to get a better angle at the door.

"Do it," Tex said as the firing became more concentrated out in the hallway. From the sound of it, Earhart and Flint were in a pitched battle.

"The bug's in that gold thing on the floor," Hawk said.

"Now it all makes sense," he said aloud.

"I'm glad," Hawk said. "Explain it to me as soon as we get out of here."

"Copy that," he said.

He reached out, grabbed the gold statue, and yanked it back to the shelter of the desk, causing a dozen more shots to pound into the carpet, desk, and walls of the office. He stuffed the statue into a pouch on his hip, letting the weight of it settle against him. Then he made sure both machine guns were fully loaded and ready.

"Flint, Earhart, position?" Tex asked.

"Inside outer office," Flint said. "We're pinned down. Can't even get a shot off."

"Frag grenades down the hallways," Tex said. "One at a time, both directions. How many do you have?"

"Three," Flint said.

"Four," Earhart answered.

"Space them," Tex said. "Make it seem like your last each time. Give 'em a chance to poke their heads out again after each one."

"Copy," Flint said.

"Hawk," Tex said, glancing over at where she was pinned down under the opening of the big window. "Got any incendiary?"

"Three," Hawk said.

"Lob them over the edge in three different directions," Tex said. "Try not to hit our ship."

"Thinking we might get lucky and hit something that will smoke?"

"We can hope," he said. "Then you can drop into stealth mode and get to the outer office."

"I'm not leaving you on this killing floor," Hawk said.

"Don't worry," Tex said, "I'm gonna be there ahead of you."

"Copy that," she said.

Out in the hallway the first grenade went off; then a moment later, another. Earhart and Flint had started to clear the path for their escape.

"Ready?" Hawk asked.

"Do it," Tex said.

"One away," Hawk said.

Bullets pounded into the room, smashing more of the shelving and wood paneling.

Then a two count later Hawk said, "Two away."

More firing. The carpet was getting ripped to shreds from all the incoming rounds.

Another two count.

"Three."

The flash of the incendiary grenade lit up the office. The echo from the explosion filled the large docking floor and rumbled louder than it should have.

Tex counted a two count, and as the second flash lit the office from out in the large cavern, he took two long and hard steps and made it to the outer office. Two shots ripped up the carpet behind him. Too little too late.

The third bright flash and rumbling explosion came from the docking chamber just as Hawk appeared beside him, dropping out of stealth mode.

Another grenade went off down the hallway to

the left, then one to the right. Both Earhart and Flint were beside the door leading out into the wide corridor.

"One more grenade, and then get ready to cover my back," Tex said. "We're goin' out the way we came in."

Earhart lobbed a frag grenade as hard as he could down the hallway to the left. Shots ripped into the wood of the doorway, but Earhart had his arm and hand back inside in plenty of time.

Tex took a deep breath. "Follow me," he said.

The grenade explosion sent a shimmer through the ground and brought dust cascading from the ceiling.

An instant after the explosion, Tex stepped into the hallway, both guns in his hands, aimed down the hall. He fired, saturating the area with what he knew was a rapidly dwindling supply of ammo. They were going to need to find some weapons along the way.

It was going to be a lot harder to get out of this place than it had been to get in; that much he was sure of.

"Explain Target Jefferson to me."

Jane Oxford sat staring at Protectorate Deputy Director Petrie. She had led him to a secure room in the Protectorate headquarters, a long distance from Petrie's own office area. He seemed very uncomfortable, sitting there, in this plain, concrete-floored room, wearing his concert-going tux and finely polished black shoes. She could see a few drops of sweat forming on his forehead.

Around them the room was stark, with only a plain aluminum table and two chairs. The room was meant to be used as an interrogation room instead of a high-level meeting room. But she wanted him to be out of his element, and this was just about as far out as Damian Petrie, the wealthy son of a privileged family, could get. She wanted him to think this kind of criminal environment might be his future, and from the look on his face, she had succeeded.

She just sat and stared at him, letting her question float in the air over the scarred tabletop.

He glanced around, then back at her. "Are you sure this room is secure?"

"One hundred percent positive," she said.

He nodded. "Then I'll hold you to that."

"Deputy Director," she said, staring at him without blinking, "at this point in time, you have no ability to hold me to anything. And unless you answer my questions directly, very soon you will not be holding your current job."

He nodded, new anger clear in his eyes. She had just backed him into a corner, and openly threatened him. All surface level civility was now gone. He would do what he needed to do to protect his position, and she knew that. She wanted it that way.

"Chancellor Jefferson runs a fairly large underground city called Kenyon, on New Bisson. Kenyon is secretive and—"

She held her hand up for him to stop. "I am aware of Kenyon, how long it has been there, and even how many people live there. I want to know why you felt it was suddenly important to kill Chancellor Jefferson."

Petrie seemed stunned at her knowledge of Kenyon. It was clear that Petrie had vastly underrated her intelligence-gathering network.

She watched as he stared at the wood tabletop between them, gathering himself. Finally Petrie said, "He had become a threat."

"To the Confederation?" she asked. "Or to you?"

"Both," he said, looking up into her eyes. She could tell it was one of the first true things he had said so far.

"Explain."

He nodded and sat back. "Kenyon, for the past two years, has been paying the Confederation a fee in return for our promise to look the other way on certain items that were being transported to their colony. Guns, some drugs, and certain alien artifacts."

"Go on," she said.

She didn't want to derail his little confession by

telling him she knew exactly how much of that "little fee" he had been keeping for himself. If that were all that concerned her, she would not be having this conversation. But something more had happened, and she didn't know what—and she didn't like not knowing.

"Chancellor Jefferson had decided the fee was too high," Petrie said, "that Kenyon had enough resources to defend its supply ships, and he wanted the fee reduced. Or done away with."

"Did you negotiate the fee?" she asked.

"No," Petrie said.

"So simply because he asked for a reduction, you felt he should be killed?"

"I felt he was gaining a little too much power, and becoming a threat to the interests of the Confed."

"And how would ten thousand people, living in a cave complex on a non-Confed world, be a threat to our interests?"

His eyes flashed anger again. She was questioning his very job, and she knew it.

"Because the information I was receiving led me to believe they were gaining too much power."

She shrugged. "So? Even if they gained enough power to topple the provisional government of New Bisson, what difference would it make? I assume Kenyon and Jefferson would be better suited to aid the Confederation than the current government of that planet, since you've been working so closely with him for so long."

He stared at her and didn't speak. For a moment she thought he might just leap across the table at her, but getting his own hands dirty wasn't his style. Her question was the very reason she was having this meeting, and she wasn't going to ease up on him until he told her the truth.

Or at least gave her a clue how to find the truth.

"It was my decision," Petrie said, his voice low and controlled, "and I stand by it."

"Oh, come on, Deputy Director," she said, shaking her head. "I need better than that."

"I deemed Chancellor Jefferson a threat, and I moved to remove the threat."

She shook her head, disgusted at the stupidity of a man who had been allowed to rise to the level of a Deputy Director in the Protectorate. The Quorum was going to have to watch itself a little more when it came to appointments; that was for sure.

She tapped a small hidden button on her wrist. A moment later the door opened, and two men, both carrying guns, stepped inside.

Director Petrie's eyes grew almost round as he saw them. She would have laughed if it hadn't been so pathetic.

"The file please," she said.

One guard handed her a paper file.

"That's all for the moment," she said.

It was her phrase for telling the guard to stay outside the door and be ready to act at once. She was just about to pull the last rug out from under Petrie's little life, and there was no telling how he would react. Having two big guards very close by was the most logical precaution she could think of.

The guards stepped back through the door and closed it.

"You think you need protection from me?" Petrie demanded.

"I am a seated Quorum member, representing the interests of an entire planet," she said, glancing through the file and ignoring the anger coming at her. "I need protection all the time."

Petrie, to his credit, said nothing more.

"Okay, Deputy Director," she said as she took a piece of paper from the file, looked at it, and then slid it across the wooden table at him.

He glanced at it, then stared, his face draining of all color.

"That, Director," she said, "is a list of your private accounts, their locations, and their current balances. Is it not?"

Still he said nothing, not even moving. For a moment she thought he might actually faint, or throw up.

"Don't worry, Deputy Director," she said, "I

have this information for every important person who works in the Protectorate branch of our fine Confederation."

His head snapped up at her, clearly surprised.

She wanted to ask him if everyone in the Protectorate branch was as stupid as he was, but she didn't.

"Normally, I would never have my attention drawn to these files. But when a mission is launched that makes no sense, and might very well end the lives of four highly trained operatives, I suddenly get interested."

He just swallowed and remained silent.

"And when twelve priceless Seer religious statues end up in a bag on your office floor, and are used as nothing more than gifts, I get even more interested."

She leaned forward and pointed to one entry near the bottom of the paper that lay in front of the deputy director. "This last deposit interests me the most. It seems to be more than all of your other account balances combined, and it came from a very interesting source. You want to tell me about it?"

He didn't even bother to look up. Clearly all the fight was gone from him. He looked like a child who had been caught breaking the rules and knew punishment was coming.

"No comment?" she asked, her voice as low

and as mean as she could make it. "Trust me, Deputy Petrie, you will want to comment. I want to know how this payment is related to the Jefferson mission. I know you pulled Confed ships from the New Bisson system. Why and where did the money come from?"

He looked up at her, the fire still in his eyes. "So you don't know everything, do you?"

"Not yet," she said. "Which is why this meeting is taking place. You tell me what's going on, and I may let you keep your job, as well as your money."

"And if I don't?" Petrie asked.

She smiled at him. "Deputy Director, you are in no position to negotiate anything. You need to tell me what I want to know."

"Or what?" Petrie asked.

"Don't push me," she said, leaning forward across the table. "You could vanish from this universe in a matter of minutes." She nodded in the direction of the door, and his face went white again.

She went on, driving her point home.

"Tomorrow morning there would be a new deputy director in your office. Your name would be forgotten almost as fast, and the coffers of my reelection fund would have gained a donation of considerable size from an unknown source as I cleared out your secret accounts. Am I clear?"

He nodded.

"So where did the money come from? And why?" She sat back and waited.

"From the Sword of Shadoon," he said, not looking at her.

That startled her. It was not the answer she was expecting at all.

Petrie went on. "Those alien nuts have something they want in the New Bisson system, on the planet with the alien ruins. They were willing to pay for the withdrawal of Confed ships and the disruption of the Kenyon colony."

She laughed. "Wow, you sure stuck it to them."

He glanced up at her, puzzled.

"You're telling me you got that much money from a bunch of Seer religious fanatics, simply because they wanted something that is buried in those alien ruins?"

"I did," he said.

"You have any idea what they are after?"

"Not yet," he said.

She nodded. She would have to get her people on it as soon as this meeting was over. But she had a few more questions for the deputy director before she let him go lick his wounds.

"So why those four operatives? Why send them into what looks like a suicide mission?"

"Tex because he found the Seer statues," Petrie said. "Flint and Hawk because they found a file that linked the Shadoon to the NRM attempt to overthrow the government on Blossom."

"I saw a copy of that file," she said, remembering how shocked she had been that the Seer cult was spreading out so far, and so fast.

"Earhart was just the pilot who could get them in."

"Not out?" she asked.

"I don't expect them to come out," Petrie said. "I've got a few agents in the Kenyon community who are in a position to retrieve dead ops chips."

She nodded. "Win-win situation for you, since you don't lose the operatives, just their memories."

"Yes, it was," Petrie said.

"All right, Deputy Director," she said, pushing herself to a standing position. "Let's take a leisurely stroll to your office and get an update on this perfect mission."

He stood, looking at her as if she were a snake that might bite him.

"Oh, come now," she said, smiling at him and opening the door, nodding to let her guards know that she was all right and that they should back off. "I know you were going to take that walk after the concert. It's still a lovely evening, and I see no reason to miss such a relaxing experience. Do you?"

"Not at all," he said, doing his best to smile as he went past her and out the door.

She laughed to herself. Maybe in an hour or so

he'd be back to his old, egotistical self, when he realized she was going to let him keep his job, his money, and his life.

At least for the moment.

Chapter Ten

The Confed rules over hundreds of planets and other settlements, in dozens of star systems, over many different races and political factions within each. At any given time, a handful of these groups are at each others' throats. Hidden within every minor, regional dispute is the seed of a conflict that could plunge the Confed into a devastating civil war.

—Jane Oxford,
Quorum delegate

Hawk did her best to hold her anger inside. She could not believe how stupid she had been, standing there and letting the target talk to her. If it hadn't been for Tex's quick action and warning, they both would be dead. And it would have been her own stupidity that would have caused it.

If she got out of this one alive, she wasn't ever going to allow that mistake to happen again. Or anything like it. A target was a target. You killed targets; you didn't talk to them.

In front of her, Tex had carved out the last opposition between Jefferson's office and the staircase they had climbed on the way in. But now the resistance had gotten thicker, and they had been forced to stop and hold at the top of the staircase. Any further delay allowed even more of the enemy to gather against them. They had to keep moving, and they all knew it.

The big circular area at the top of the staircase was not an easy area to defend, either. Guards were below them, firing up the stairs. Others were tucked into stone alcoves down three separate hallways that branched off the area.

Tex had taken a position near the staircase and was spraying minigun fire at any green-suited guard stupid enough to stick a gun or a head out into the open.

She held the position to the left of the staircase, behind a stone column, taking single shots to pick off the resistance, one kill at a time.

Earhart and Flint were to Tex's left, doing the same thing.

The sound in the massive stone area was intense, like being inside a thunderstorm. Bullets from the different rifles ricocheted from the stone, sending sparks in all directions. Her armor had been hit three times, but it had held so far. Flint had blood coming from the side of her neck, but wasn't seeming to notice, and Tex was bleeding from a scalp wound and a neck wound.

She had to do something to get them moving, and she had to do it quickly.

"I'm going stealth and down the stairs," she

said. "When you get my signal, flash them with some grenades and follow me at a full run."

"Copy that," Flint said.

Tex only nodded as she flicked on her stealth mode and took out her Powerblade. The blade could cut through just about any armor, and while she was in stealth mode, it was as invisible as she was.

She stuck to the wall to try to keep any stray shot from catching her, and took the stairs two at a time. About a dozen defenders were at the bottom, in the open, firing upward at anything that moved. They had formed a sort of line at the bottom of the staircase, blocking it. Since they were so focused on firing up, they hadn't seen her shimmering ghost image that showed up slightly when she was in stealth mode.

She went between two of them without either noticing her, then slipped in behind the one on the far right wall. Using her blade she cut his throat, then the next one in line, and then the next, all before the first one even hit the ground.

The last two posed different problems. They had noticed that their comrades were falling, and they turned. Once she had attracted their attention, she had no doubt they could see her shimmering, waterlike movement. One raised a rifle straight at her, but she ducked under his line and sliced him in half.

At that moment the power pack on her stealth

mode ran out, and she was visible again. Luckily, the one remaining guard didn't have time to react, and she cut his head off with one slash of her blade.

As the head of the last guard rolled on the stone floor of the large hallway, she shouted, "Clear!"

Then she tucked in behind a stone pillar, got out her rifle, and did a quick scan of the area. Four green-suited guards were heading her way at full run, right up the middle of Parkway, their laser rifles carried at their sides. They must not have noticed the guards down at the bottom of the stairs yet, since the firing was still intense at the top.

She picked one off at a hundred paces, took out the second as he skidded to a stop, caught the third in the head as he ducked for cover, and missed with her fourth shot, but killed him with her fifth shot before he got to cover and tried to fire back.

Above her a number of grenades shook the stone and sent dust swirling through the air.

Tex was first to head down the stairs, his bulk pounding the ground as he ran, the machine gun in his hands steady and ready to fire.

"I'm on the right wall going down Parkway," Hawk told him, breaking out of her cover after killing another guard who had made the mistake of stepping onto Parkway two hundred paces away. "At the moment our road is clear in both directions."

Another grenade shook the stone under her feet.

"Clear," Flint said, bursting over the top and taking the stairs three at a time.

Hawk was impressed. Flint didn't usually move that fast, but this time she managed a good speed and was at the bottom of the staircase not more than a few steps behind Tex.

More firing, and then another two grenades went off.

"Clear. On the stairs, as well," Earhart said as he started down lumbering a lot more than Flint had done, yet still making good time. He looked to Hawk as if he must have taken a hit in the right leg, since he was favoring it.

Hawk got to the right wall as Tex went left off the bottom of the stairs.

Flint, right behind him, went right at the bottom.

Earhart was about halfway down when the firing began from above, heavy and fast.

Flint dived and rolled, coming up quickly with her back against a rock wall. She then turned, offering Earhart cover fire.

Tex had also stopped, and was spraying the open area at the top of the staircase with round after round from both his machine guns.

Hawk tried to move to get into position to offer Earhart cover, as well, but she was too late.

Earhart, caught in the middle of the open staircase, didn't fare well in the barrage of fire from above. From what Hawk could tell, three or four shots caught him squarely in the back, jerking his head back, then forward. He lost his grip on his rifle and tumbled down the stone staircase like a sack of flour, head-over-heels, three times. The enemy fire stopped abruptly when Flint's expertly placed frag grenade went off in their midst, but the damage was done.

The moment Earhart's tumble stopped, two steps from the bottom, it was clear to Hawk that he was dead. Blood streamed from what had been the lower half of his face. A bullet must have entered the back of his neck and exploded out the front.

She stared at their dead pilot. Her worst fear had come true. Suddenly, with one shot, their escape plans had changed.

They were now in backup mode, and all three of them knew it at once. The ship they had come in on would not be taking them out of this mountain. Earhart had been the only one of them who could fly it well enough to make that tricky path of escape work. On the way down, Flint had referred to their backup plan as the "ditch and pray" option.

They now faced a trio of disturbing unknowns: finding a way out, surviving whatever the remaining forces might throw at them in the mountains, and hoping Commander Seton would send a pickup team that could competently find them and safeguard their exit.

Hawk glanced at her watch. Sixteen minutes into the operation. In one hour and forty-four minutes, the inside of this mountain would become a radioactive ruin when the core of their ship exploded. Nothing would survive in any of these tunnels, including them.

"Earhart is dead," Hawk said. "Ditch."

"And pray," Tex said, agreeing, his voice low even over the comm link. "Get his chip."

Hawk knelt by Earhart with her claw already in hand, and ran her left thumb through the hair at the back of his head until she found the socket. In one smooth motion she hooked the pull-catch of the chip, jerked the claw forward to pop it free, and pulled it out with her left hand. She stood, slipped the chip into a pocket on her thigh, and turned to head up the wide, high-ceiling tunnel called Parkway, away from their ship, away from the coming explosion.

Unlike her last mission, where she lost two good ops forever, at least Earhart had a decent chance of being cloned and brought back. Which meant now she was carrying not only her own life, but Earhart's life, as well.

Ten thousand people were going to die very

shortly, and at the moment she didn't want to think about that. She couldn't let herself think about what that explosion was going to do.

At a run, Tex and Flint moved out with her, deserting both the shell that moments ago had been Earhart and the last hope that anyone in this mountain would live to see fresh air and sunlight again.

"You did what?" Deputy Director Petrie demanded.

Commander Seton, the controller in charge of the Jefferson op, leaned back away from his screen and from the anger of the Deputy Director. Jane Oxford sat off to one side in Director Petrie's plush, overfurnished office, out of the line of sight of the vid link, listening to the conversation. She didn't like what she was hearing.

"We set the ship to blow if they didn't get out," Commander Seton said. "We figured if they failed to get their target, the ship's core explosion would finish the job."

Petrie sort of sputtered and said nothing, his head shaking from side to side.

Oxford couldn't believe what she was hearing. It seemed that if the pilot was killed, or all of the operatives were killed, or captured, the ten thousand people who lived in that mountain would also be killed. If that was the case, they were facing a crisis of proportions she didn't want to think about.

"You're an idiot," Petrie said.

"You said you wanted the target taken out at all costs," Seton said.

"Operative costs," Petrie said, his voice soft. "Operative costs."

Seton said nothing.

Oxford had no doubt that the problem wasn't just with Seton, but with Petrie, as well.

"Report to me in my office at once, when you get word of mission progress."

"I will," Seton said.

Petrie cut the connection and looked over at her. She could tell he was not happy with what might happen.

"It seems to me your win-win situation just became a big loser," she said, "if those operatives don't pull off the impossible and get that ship out of there."

"They're good," Petrie said.

"Let's hope so," she said, standing and starting to pace. "But right now we have to assume they don't make it, and that place blows up. I do understand that's what's going to happen. Am I right?"

The expression on his face showed that Petrie clearly didn't like the thought, but he nodded.

"So we're going to have a political mess on our hands the likes of which I've never seen before."

"New Bisson is not a Confed world. There was a tragic accident. No survivors. Nothing more."

"Except for the possibility of operatives who get out ahead of the explosion," she said. "And those who knew what really happened there." She pointed at the vid screen, indicating the controller, Seton.

He nodded, understanding what she was saying. "You also knew they were going in."

"I did," she said. "And that means others at my level knew, as well, I'm sure. Killing a few political heads of a revolt-minded organization is one thing. Wiping out an entire city of people is a matter that can have a lot of weight."

"Too much weight," he said, sitting back in his ego-size chair and putting his hands over his face.

She could tell he was slowly starting to understand the full ramifications of what was happening.

"Exactly," she said. "In the political landscape of the Quorum, the balance is uneasy at best. Every world imagines it could go it alone just fine. Almost anything could tip the Confederation into a war among member planets, a war that would be impossible for us to contain. And killing a city full of people is one of those events that might upset the scales, if the news gets out."

Petrie sat forward and stared at her, his eyes intense and cold.

"So we make sure we have under control everyone who knows about this mission," Petrie said.

She laughed, thinking about the older, ex-operative who had told her about it. There was no telling how many others knew.

"Not likely," she said. "Let's just hope those operatives are as good as we think they are."

Chapter Eleven

Operatives have to work on their own, each thinking for the team, each leading and following at the same time. A top team functions perfectly when all are in charge.

—Kisor,
operative training, day one

They were two hundred paces up the large, wide, high-ceiling cavern the Kenyon residents called Parkway, headed away from their original point of entry, when Tex finally made up his mind.

The backup plan called for them to take a tunnel a few hundred paces ahead of their current location, to a side staircase, then up four levels, along another tunnel, to an air access system, then into the ventilation system where they would work their way out the side of the mountain and get as far away as possible before the ship blew.

But the image of those two frightened secretaries sticking their heads out of the door, screaming and jumping back, bothered him. They were just two of the ten thousand people who lived here. Jefferson had been their target, not those secretaries. The target was terminated, and the mission a success. But because of the wrong person getting killed, ten thousand people were going to die, and die facing the heat and torture of what he had faced not so long ago on Dower.

"No!" Tex said, stopping cold and moving to one side in order to take up a defensive position with his back against the stone of the wall. Since the security forces seemed convinced that the team's destination was the shuttle, they likely had concentrated there. So the team had run into very little resistance since leaving the staircase, and at the moment none was in sight.

"No what?" Flint asked. "Why are we stopping?" She moved over and pressed against a column that allowed her cover.

Hawk faded into a rock alcove.

"No," Tex said, "I'm sorry, but we can't let ten thousand people die."

There was silence over the communication link.

He couldn't see either Flint's or Hawk's face, and he had no idea how they were reacting, so he went on. "We killed the target; the mission is finished. There's no need to trigger the backup."

"Do you know how to get into that ship and disarm the bomb?" Flint's voice in his ear was hard. "I don't. We both know that just trying will get you killed by setting off the bomb early. So I say we keep moving. We have no choice. We save ourselves."

"I know my way around explosives, I've disarmed devices before, and I paid attention when Seton and Earhart discussed the arming sequence." Tex kept his tone level. "I can't fly the ship, but I think I can disarm the bomb."

"If we're parked in one spot, guarding your back while you do this, we'll need all your firepower just to keep them off us," Flint replied.

The link again fell silent for agonizing seconds.

"We go back," Hawk finally said. "I'll take the ship, Tex will stand guard with you, and he'll talk me through the disarming sequence. I didn't like the idea of killing this many innocent people, either."

"Soft touches," Flint said. "You know this is going to get us all killed."

"Yeah, I know," Hawk said.

"Worth the shot," Tex said.

And he believed it. The target was gone. They had no orders to kill everyone else in these caves. And the memory of that core explosion on Dower was still far, far too fresh in his mind. He felt relief flood in at the thought that they might be able to stop this.

"Hawk, take point," Flint said. "Tex, you follow her. I'll cover your asses."

"By my watch, we have one hour and twenty minutes," Hawk said.

"Plenty of time to get us killed," Tex said.

"Let's try to not let that happen," Flint said.

"Good idea," Hawk said.

"One more idea," Hawk said as she started out, moving silently along the wall headed back down Parkway. "Tex, give us a rundown of how to disarm that bomb as we go. I want to have a fighting chance at it, if you get killed."

"Thanks for the morale boost," Tex said. "I'm going to do my best to stay alive."

"You're welcome," Hawk said.

Tex stepped out into the open and followed Hawk, both his miniguns fully loaded, one on his shoulder, the other aimed forward.

Flint raised her rifle in midstride and picked off two guards in green uniforms who had been heading their way as Tex started, step by step, to give Hawk and Flint a crash course on what he knew about disarming the trigger that would set off the core explosion.

"Nothing yet, sir," Commander Seton reported.

"It's going on one hour," Deputy Director Petrie said.

"I know," Seton said. His tone indicated he was not happy with being grilled. "They have two hours from the time they left the ship to get back before the bomb goes off."

Petrie glanced over at where Jane Oxford sat, watching the conversation. He didn't like having her in his office, but she showed no signs of leaving until this was settled.

"But the main schedule had them in and out in thirty minutes," Petrie said. "Am I correct?"

"You are, sir," Seton said, "but operatives are a very independent bunch. They tend to think and act on their own. I said I'll call you once they report in. Until then, there's nothing I can do."

"Make sure you do call," Petrie said, and cut the vid link.

What had started out being one of the better nights of his life had turned so ugly, even he hadn't yet grasped all the implications. Jane Oxford, Quorum delegate, knew everything he did. He had no idea how his security could have been breached so completely, but it had. There was no telling how many others knew about his business.

Now, because of an idiot backup plan fashioned by a moron of a controller, he had no doubt that if that bomb went off in Kenyon, his life wouldn't be worth the chair he was sitting on.

"It seems, Deputy Director," Oxford said, "that we are getting closer to having a real problem."

"I agree," Petrie said. "Any ideas?" At this point, his only choice was to agree with her and try to work with her. And then hope to survive the backlash that was sure to come from all sides, including inside the Protectorate branch.

"Do you have a notepad of some sort?" Oxford asked.

He opened the top drawer of his desk and pulled one out. He slid it across the surface at her.

She pushed it back at him. "I want you to make a list of everyone who you think might know about this mission, including the operatives."

He took out a favorite pen. "These missions are supposed to be of utmost secrecy," he said. "I had no idea you even knew about it."

"I know that," she said. "Just write.

He put down the four operatives' names, his name, Seton's name, and her name. "Seven, counting you and me."

"Add Banson to the list," she said.

"The retired operative?" he asked as he wrote. Petrie had no idea how Banson could have known. He hadn't been on the active list for a few years. Clearly he had been working other duties, though.

"Yes, he was the one who told me about it," Oxford said. "We'll have to find out who else he told, and who else Seton told."

Petrie looked at the list. He had no doubt it was going to get longer. And the longer it got, the uglier this got, as if killing ten thousand people wasn't ugly enough.

"So now we wait," Oxford said. "Any chance you have something to drink in this office?"

"You don't know?" he asked.

"I didn't plan on ever coming here, Deputy Director," she said, smiling at him.

He had no doubt that if she had, she would have known exactly where he kept his scotch.

Tex was getting damned tired of the big stone corridor they called Parkway. He'd seen the sights, the trees, the grass, the bodies once before. He didn't really want to be here anymore, but it had been his idea to go back, and he was going to see it through.

The resistance had turned nasty right as Tex got past the staircase. It confirmed that the guards had expected them to make a move toward their ship.

He was down to a few hundred rounds of ammunition, so he ditched one of his machine guns and picked up a laser cannon.

Fully charged.

He swung his last remaining machine gun over his shoulder and aimed the laser cannon down Parkway at a cluster of guards. The cannon worked almost as well as his favorite minis.

Flint and Hawk moved up under his covering fire and got into position, Hawk against the left wall, Flint against the right. From there they could pick off any guard who poked a head out when Tex stopped firing.

It was a method they had used a number of times, and for the moment it seemed to be working yet again.

Parkway had become a graveyard over the last hour. With all the guards they had killed on the way up to the target, and now the pitched fight going back, the blood was flowing. But not as much as would flow if he, Flint, and Hawk didn't win this battle.

"Grenade!" Flint shouted.

Tex was walking, step by step, down the slightly inclined tunnel, staying to the middle near the cover of the stone benches and grass and trees. That center line allowed him full range of fire ahead. Flint was on the left, Hawk on the right, both watching his back and picking off targets from long range and between bursts of his fire.

The grenade Flint had shouted about came from down the corridor. It was the first time the defenders had taken to using explosives. That wasn't a good sign for things to come.

Tex dropped to the ground and rolled to his left against a stone bench as the grenade bounced once and then went off twenty paces in front of him.

The concussion rang his eardrums, and a splinter of stone cut his cheek, but otherwise he was fine.

A single shot rang out as the blast echoed off into the distance.

"I got the joker who threw that," Hawk said as Tex climbed back to one knee and fired the laser cannon down the corridor, a spread of beams melting holes in the plants and sending two green-suited guards to their chosen afterlives.

He had just got back to his feet and had taken two more steps when Flint yelled "Grenade."

He dropped again, this time rolling to the left onto the lawn.

The frag blew up about fifteen paces behind him, yet again ringing his ears, but it accomplished nothing else.

"Got that one, too," Flint said.

"This is gonna get old, people," Tex said.

"Already is," Hawk said.

Again Tex came up firing, spraying the hallway ahead, not allowing any of the green-suited guards to get an open shot at any of them.

Or throw any more grenades.

One guy tried and lost his head and an arm in the process. His dropped grenade exploded and killed his buddy tucked into a rock alcove beside him.

Tex could see the side corridor just twenty paces ahead. Getting down that narrow, low-ceiling tunnel and into the ship was going to be another bit of very unpleasant work.

Then once in the ship, giving Hawk enough time and cover to get the trigger defused was going to be even tougher. Too bad he just couldn't tell these people the truth, that they were trying to save the lives of everyone in the place. Somehow Tex doubted they would believe him.

Tex studied the opening that led into that tunnel. There was nothing there at all that provided cover. Nothing that would allow them to defend the mouth of that passageway. They either had to defend it from where they were, or go all the way to the ship.

Tex didn't like the sound of going to the ship. Enemy shots down the tunnel would simply bounce off the stone, until they went out the other end or hit something solid. And there wasn't much solid in that tunnel, so it would be like funneling shots right into the ship's hatch. Allowing fire to be directed into that side tunnel would be the worst thing they could do.

Flint picked off two guards with two quick shots.

Tex caught another one who had wandered too far out in the open, with a beam that cut off one leg and left the man screaming on the stone.

Hawk fired three times, right in a row, back up the corridor, and another guard's screams joined the chorus of pain.

"Flint," Tex said, "we need to hold up right where we are at." Tex glanced around and stopped. There was a stone bench a few feet from him that he could use for cover, if he needed.

"I'm in a good defensive position," Flint said. "I'll stop here."

Tex glanced over at where Flint had taken up a spot behind a rock ledge and had shoved her body back and almost out of sight. It allowed her to have a clear shot at almost anything in either direction, up or down the wide corridor.

"Agreed," Hawk said. "Let them think they've got us stopped here. My stealth mode is recharged, so I'll go into the corridor first. I'll have a better chance of making it that way. I haven't seen anyone come out of that hallway in a while, so I think they all tried to stop us out here."

"Makes sense," Flint said.

"We'll keep the entrance of that side tunnel clear for you," Tex said. "Just don't be too long."

"Back before you know I'm gone," Hawk said, flipping on her stealth field and vanishing.

Tex blasted at a number of guards who seemed to be gaining some courage about a hundred paces down the corridor, then moved over and up-ended the stone bench, shoving it away from the grass and out onto the rock floor.

There was another stone bench ten feet away. Firing as he went at three green-suited idiots who had decided to make a move to a safer location closer to him, he got to the other stone bench before the three bodies stopped twitching.

He yanked the bench loose and moved out beside the other one, putting the legs of the benches together to form a protected square space right in the middle of the corridor. That gave him a stone front shield, and stone back shield.

Tex stepped over one bench and into his little fort as Flint fired at a guy trying to run to a better position down the corridor. Tex sat down inside his makeshift stone protection, his mini resting on one stone bench and aiming down the corridor, and the laser cannon resting on the other bench, aiming up the corridor.

He took turns, spraying the corridor first up the hill and then down.

With Flint picking them off at long range, he kept the closer ones in check. He had no doubt they could hold this position for a short time. The question was, how long?

If it took Hawk even a few seconds more than fifty-one minutes, it wasn't going to matter anyway.

A guy in a green suit holding a grenade stepped into the open and reared back to throw it. Flint took off his hand with a single, perfect shot. Tex was impressed. What would he give for that kind of precision? Might be worth becoming half machine.

The grenade, with the guy's hand still attached, rolled back and exploded, taking out two other guards hiding in a side corridor.

Tex kept firing, first up the corridor, then down the corridor. A few moments later Hawk said, "I'm in. Now comes the fun part."

"Take your time," Tex said, firing up the corridor from his stone bench fort. "We're not going anywhere."

Chapter Twelve

Sure, you're trained to do certain things, equipped for certain tasks. But once you're in the middle of an op, you find yourself doing all kinds of things you didn't expect, under fire, and with no time. What choice do you have? The cavalry isn't going to show up to save your sorry ass.

—Pyne,
Expose journal entry

Hawk let the hatch of the ship close, then locked it, and dropped her rifle on the carpet of the shuttle. The ship had once been a corporate transport ship, sparse and fast, used for private flights between corporate headquarters on one world and the offices on another. It was highly maneuverable and, as Earhart had proved, could land anywhere, in almost any conditions. It wasn't as plush as some of the ships she had been on, but it wasn't bad. If she hadn't been so worried about the mission, she might have enjoyed the flight that had brought them to New Bisson.

She could feel the engine of the fine craft still humming on standby. No Kenyon guard had tried to tamper with the ship, and there had been no guard posted outside it. She guessed the people in charge felt that once the intruders were eliminated, there would be more than enough time to deal with the extra ship.

A slight miscalculation.

She glanced at her watch. Forty-two minutes left. She had never been on a mission that had lasted this long. Normally they were in and out, surgical strikes that were carefully timed. Everything about this mission was going sour; that was for sure.

She went down the short aisle, past the bathroom, and to a panel in the back wall. Tex had told her what to look for. It was some sort of fake wood, almost oak in color. She yanked the panel loose and tossed it aside, then ducked into the engine compartment.

There the sounds of the engine were louder, more of a rumbling. The compartment was warm, with a metal floor and walls. At the back end of the ship was the drive and core. It looked like an impossible jumble of wires, intermixed with readout monitors and metal faceplates. Earhart had set the bomb's trigger from the cockpit, but Tex had said it had to be disarmed at the engine.

"Grenade!" Flint shouted over the comm link.

"Got it!" Tex replied.

The ground shook a little, but inside the ship it felt like only a slight bump. Flint and Tex could be overrun at any moment. She needed to find the trigger Tex had described, get this done, and get out of here.

Hawk forced herself to take a deep breath. The air was stale and smelled of the lubricant she had used when working on her rifle. The mass of equipment in front of her looked like an alien being that might come alive and swallow her at any moment.

"Calm down," she said under her breath.

"Easy for you to say," Tex said, "but out here they've decided to start tossin' more grenades. You find it yet?"

She smiled. "Sorry—talking to myself. Still looking."

"Just hope I'm around to help you with it," Tex said. Then a moment later he said, "Grenade!"

Again the ground shook slightly under the ship.

"Let's start pickin' them off before they throw those things," Tex said.

"Copy that," Flint said.

Hawk squinted and tried to reconcile Tex's terse description of the trigger mechanism with the jumbled, technological chaos that lay before her. After a couple of minutes of scrutiny, she knew she needed to try something else. She relaxed, let her gaze take in the whole scene, visualized the shape of the trigger, and willed that shape to emerge from the confusion.

It worked. The trigger that would set off the

core was in front of her, just as Tex described. She quickly moved to it. "All right, Tex, I'm ready."

"First, open the blue panel," he said.

"Blue panel," she said aloud, following the instructions.

"Second, unhook the top anchor wire from the chip board plate."

She found the anchor wire and unhooked it.

A burst of gunfire rang through the comm link. After a moment, Tex's voice returned. "Now pull out the center chip board."

She pulled the board, holding the three-inch square in her hand.

"Next, turn the board one hundred and eighty degrees and replace it."

She did that, her hands shaking slightly.

She paused, and then drew both hands from the board.

Nothing exploded.

If she had remembered everything correctly, the core would be fine. She headed out of the engine room, up the short aisle, and into the cockpit. There, beside the pilot's seat was a digital read-out, frozen at forty-one minutes and sixteen seconds.

"Countdown halted," she said, aloud.

"Confirmed?" Flint asked.

"Confirmed," Hawk said.

There was a long pause; then Tex said, "Well done."

"Well done." Flint repeated.

Those were the best two words Hawk had heard in some time.

"Thanks," she said. "Anyone need some ammunition out there, since I'm in here?"

They both laughed.

"I'll take that as an affirmative," she said.

She was about to leave the cockpit when a motion caught her eye. Out the shuttle's window she could see part of the floor of the big interior landing area. The Kenyons had clearly scrambled to get a couple of their fighter ships ready to launch. She could see two atmospheric defenders, heavily armed, standing by, as well.

At that moment, for the first time since Earhart had been killed, she thought about what they were going to do next to get out of this mission alive. If they did take the backup plan escape route, they would end up on the surface, among the rocks and cliffs that made up the ground above this cavern complex. Then they would have to call for pickup. It would be hours coming. And no way would the pickup ship stand a chance against those fighters sitting down there.

"We have another problem," Hawk said, easing as far forward as she could to see through the cockpit window without giving her position away.

"We're waitin' breathlessly," Tex said.

"From here," Hawk said, "I can see two atmosphere fighters warmed up and ready to launch, plus two deep-space ships that look heavily armed and ready to launch, as well."

"You weren't kiddin' about the problem," Tex said.

"We won't stand a chance outside this mountain unless we disable those ships," Flint said, stating the only solution that Hawk could see, as well.

"How far are they from your position?" Tex asked.

"One hundred meters," she said, studying the distance between her and adjusting for the drop. With a rifle, she could take out any worker around those ships. But that wouldn't stop the ships from launching.

"How close are they parked together?" Tex asked.

"Close," Hawk said, staring through the window. "Took some good piloting to get them in those berths. What are you thinking?"

"We have two choices," Tex said. "You try to take them out from there, or we fight our way down there and try to take them out up close."

"How about we hijack one with a pilot?" Flint asked.

"Too risky," Hawk said. "Plus we'd have to get the damn dome open, as well."

"Agreed," Tex said. "We stick with the escape route and try to take those ships out first."

"I've got two rocket launchers here in the ship," Hawk said. She had almost no training on using them, but she didn't mention that.

"Take a look the other way," Tex said.

"What way?" Hawk said, glancing around to see if anyone was coming at her down the corridor. Then across the cavern at the far wall.

"Up," Tex said. "Anything above those ships a missile might bring down?"

"Oh," she said. "Hang on."

"Trust me," Tex said. "We're not goin' anywhere. I'm thinkin' of having mail delivered."

Hawk moved around to the other side of the small cockpit and put her head down on the seat so she could look up at the roof of the cavern. The huge door was closed. It was made of a dull metal and was suspended on both sides with large beams dug into the rock sides of the cavern. A missile fired against the rock under those beams just might cause the entire roof structure to collapse and bury the ships. Nothing would be launching out of that kind of mess.

"Good thinking," Hawk said. "I'm going to try to bring the roof down."

"Grenade!" Flint said.

The explosion shook the ship slightly.

"You know how to use a launcher?" Flint asked.

"I'll get by," Hawk said. "I can always check instructions with you two." She was half joking, half afraid she might have to do just that.

"We'll keep you covered," Tex said, ignoring her attempt at humor. "But bring supplies when you come."

"Copy that," she said. "I'll move them into the tunnel first, just in case something happens to me or the ship."

"Understood," Tex said.

"Grenade!" Flint said.

Again the explosion shook the ship as Hawk moved back and began working through the extra supplies of ammunition, guns, and missile launchers they had brought with them.

Commander Dan Arington, head of Kenyon security, stepped over the dead body of Chancellor Jefferson's secretary and moved into what was left of the chancellor's office. The shelves were down, the desk was riddled with bullet holes, and the carpet was torn up as if a wild animal had dug at it.

Arington, taking shallow breaths through his mouth to avoid the stink of death, moved around the desk. Most of the chancellor's body had been tossed backwards out of his chair and into a bloody pile. His head lay to one side, and his neck and upper chest were no more than hunks of flesh splattered on the wall and out the broken window.

The big guy with the machine guns must have cut the chancellor in half with a simultaneous blast from both guns. Clearly Jefferson had been their target. They had come in, made a direct line to Jefferson's office, and then left.

Jefferson had made the stupid mistake of not going to the safe bunker when Arington had told him to. If he had, he would be alive now.

"Commander."

He turned away from the bloody mess and tapped the comm link on his collar. "Go ahead."

"We have them stopped just short of the corridor that leads to their ship." It was Lieutenant Davis, one of highest ranking men he had left. The four above him had been killed at various points along the firefight.

"Stopped?" Arington asked.

"Yes," the lieutenant said. "The large one is crouched between two stone benches, one woman is tucked into a rock alcove, and we think the third is dead."

"But you're not sure?" Arington asked.

"No, sir," the lieutenant said.

Arington didn't like the sound of that at all. "How far from the corridor for the executive ship platform?"

"Twenty paces is all," the lieutenant said.

"I think they're concerned we'll trap them down that hallway."

Arington didn't like the sound of that either. These people, whoever they were, did not seem like the kind who would stay pinned down for long. Or worry about being trapped. They had the best armor, the highest-tech weapons, and the smarts of a well-trained unit. He hadn't seen anything like it since his days in the service of the Confed.

Maybe, just maybe, what he and his men were facing was one of the rumored special ops teams. It would make sense. Jefferson, who sometimes didn't understand the art of graceful silence, more than likely had made someone in the Confed angry. And this was the response. People who went against the Confed for too long tended to end up dead or missing.

"Don't make a move on them until I arrive," he said.

"Yes, sir," the lieutenant said.

Arington turned and faced what was left of Jefferson. "You dumb bastard. Who did you piss off?"

Arington then turned and headed out, back into the carnage of the hallway, where the medical staff was trying to save the still living. There weren't many.

If he was facing a special ops team, then that team had to be thinking of a way out right about now. Why would they have gone back to their ship area? They couldn't fly out with the cargo bay door closed. Going back there made no sense to him.

He wound his way at a fast walk down the corridor, weaving in and around the bodies strewn everywhere. If he lost only a hundred men today, he would be lucky. More than likely the total would go much higher. Four of them with one or two casualties versus a hundred of his men lost.

This was one hard team he was facing. And a team like this one didn't move or act without thought and plan. He reached the top of the staircase and looked around.

So why had they gone down the staircase and right at the bottom, away from their ship. That was the path he would have expected them to take if they were trying to get out of the mountain on foot.

But then they turned around and went back. Why? He knew for a fact they had not been lost.

He moved to the bottom of the staircase. A good distance down Parkway the shooting continued, usually single shots, but once in a while there was a thundering blast from one of the big man's machine guns.

Arington stayed against the wall, inside the stair alcove, and studied the situation, trying to think like one of the operatives trapped down there.

Why did they go up Parkway, then change their minds and move down to a spot near their ship? But then stop and not go into the ship.

Unless the third member was still alive and had somehow gotten on the ship without his men seeing her. He had walked around their ship when his men had had the team stopped at the top of the stairs, saw no weapons ports, and decided the ship could wait. Suddenly he regretted that decision. He should have blown it off the platform when he had the chance.

Stupid mistake. He was making a number of them today.

He glanced around at the body of the member of the team they had killed. He had no identification on him, and his weapons could have been bought anywhere. Maybe it was this man's death that had caused them to go up Parkway first and then change plans.

Arington stood over the body. "Are you their pilot?"

Suddenly the pieces were starting to fall in place. They had decided to try to walk out when this guy was killed, then changed their minds and went back to their ship, more than likely to reload and then work to capture a pilot, and one of the Kenyon ships now standing by. They still hoped to fly out of here. With his fighter ships, they must have realized they had no chance on foot outside the mountain.

"Thanks," he said to the dead body at his feet. Then he touched his comm link. "Lieutenant."

"Yes, sir," the lieutenant said.

"I want everyone to fall back to the doors around the cargo bay."

"And leave the invaders?" the lieutenant asked.

"Do as I say, son," Arington said, his voice harsh.

"Yes, sir," the lieutenant said.

Arington went on with his orders. "Then I want snipers back on the walls of the cargo bay and all ships' pilots taken out of the bay to a secure location."

"Yes, sir," the lieutenant said.

"Leave just one man to trail the invading team, but do not engage unless they approach those cargo bay doors," Arington said. "Repeat, do not engage."

"Understood," the lieutenant said.

Arington smiled. Two could play this game. He held all the cards. He would let them walk out without losing another man, and his pilots would blow them off the side of the mountain.

And if they tried to get into the cargo bay and take a ship, they would die trying. If that little ship tried to lift off, it wouldn't last two seconds.

He turned and headed back up the staircase. It would take him a few extra minutes to go through tunnels that wound over Parkway, to get around the shooters and down into the cargo bay. But he had no doubt, he had the time.

* * *

"They're pulling back," Flint said as she pulled off another shot, killing a man two hundred paces down the corridor as he tried to dash for new cover.

"Why?" Tex asked, feeling as surprised as Flint sounded. In front of him it was obvious the green-suited guards were moving back, not up, one cover location at a time.

He glanced around at Parkway going toward the staircase. What few soldiers who had been back up that way were also pulling back.

"Reloads in the corridor," Hawk said. "I'm pulling out a couple missile launchers."

"Maybe they're going to bomb this area," Flint said.

Tex watched as three green-suited men, far out of his machine-gun range, made a dash for safety into a side corridor. Flint didn't even bother to take a shot at them.

"What are they up to?" Flint asked.

"I don't know," he said. He had a very bad feeling about this. Very bad. "But we're goin' to have to move fast."

"I'm almost ready in here," Hawk said.

"Get out two extra missiles," Tex said. "I'll fire two; you fire two."

"Copy that," Hawk said. "Glad to have the help."

"Keep an eye out," Tex said to Flint.

"I'll keep two," she said.

He jumped up and out of the little stone fort that had protected him the last few minutes and at a full run went into the side corridor.

Up ahead he could see another mini and the pile of extra ammunition for his guns and Flint's. Plus some extra grenades to restock what they had used. Hawk was just inside the corridor, using the bulk of the ship as a shield to hide her activities.

As Tex skidded to a stop beside her she handed him a rocket launcher. "Loaded. Thermalite. That ought to punch a hole in that roof's support system."

"We can hope," Tex said.

"Aim right at where the big roof beam goes into the rock," Hawk said. "That has to be the weakest point."

Tex nodded, picking up the second missile so that he'd have it close to him for a fast reload. "I'll go to the right of the ship."

Hawk nodded. "It would be better if you did the shooting."

Tex glanced at his scout, who only shrugged. "I'll feed them to you, but as I said, I've never really been trained on these things before."

"Makes sense," Tex said. "You hand them to me one right after another. I'm goin' to alternate from left to right, as fast as I can."

"Understand," Hawk said, dropping the launcher and picking up the two missiles, then taking the third from Tex.

"Let's do it," Tex said.

Tex led them out of the corridor, going right around the back of the small shuttle. He stepped just far enough into the open to get a clear shot at the beam, pulled the missile launcher up on his shoulder, and fired.

The missile streaked at the beam, where it entered the rock cliff and exploded.

Hawk handed him a second, and he had it loaded and fired in a matter of seconds.

The second missile exploded right where he had aimed it.

She handed him a third, and he fired again.

This time his target was clouded by smoke and dust, but he got a good spot on the general area from the first firing.

A bullet pinged off the ship right beside his head.

One more. Hawk handed him the last missile and set up cover fire.

He got a bead through the dust and smoke overhead and fired; then he dropped the missile launcher and moved back for cover as more shots bounced off the ship and rocks around them. One slammed into his shoulder, spinning him around, but leaving him standing. Luckily his armor had taken most of that hit, or he would have been down for the count.

As Tex's last missile exploded overhead there was a tremendous rumble. Then the shrieking of metal being torn apart filled the cavern.

"Back!" Tex shouted.

He got through the opening of the tunnel a half second ahead of Hawk. Behind them it sounded like the entire world was being torn apart. The ground shook hard, bouncing their extra ammunition.

Metal scraped against metal, dust swirled and filled the air. From the sounds of it, they had brought the roof down. The ships in that cargo bay wouldn't be going anywhere fast.

He grabbed most of the ammunition clips and grenades and headed down the short corridor at a full run. The force of the wind as the big roof fell, compressing everything in its way, shoved him from behind like a hand against his back.

"Got the rest," Hawk shouted.

Tex hit the open air of Parkway and went left toward his stone bench fort, dropping the ammunition and grenades inside and then turning, both miniguns back in his hands.

"No action out here," Flint said.

Hawk had gotten away from the blast of dust and smoke coming from the hallway they had just been in. It looked like it was coming out under pressure.

The ground shook hard under his feet; dust and some rock fell from the ceiling. There was no doubt the falling roof door had taken out their small ship on the way down, as well.

"Now's the time to get moving," Hawk said.

"Agreed," Tex said as the dust quickly filled the wide corridor, rolling in clouds in both directions. He grabbed two extra bundles of ammunition and slung them over his shoulder, then took the grenades he needed to replace the ones he had used.

Hawk appeared out of the dust beside him, then Flint. Within seconds Flint had the supplies she needed and was ready to move.

"Spread out," Tex said. "At a jog. Hawk, take point."

"Copy that," Hawk said, turning and vanishing almost instantly into the swirling dust and smoke.

Tex set off behind her, one machine gun in his hands, another over his shoulder. He stayed to the middle of Parkway, moving at a steady jog.

He knew and trusted that Flint would be a distance behind him, on the left. They all knew where they were going, and now, for the first time, maybe they had a chance of making it.

Chapter Thirteen

To the operative, the controller is the sole point of contact, planning, and supply in an op. Few operatives appreciate how directly their fates are tied to the infighting between controllers, for the best operatives and the most lucrative assignments.

—Constance Bell,
Deputy Director of Operations, Region Five

Petrie stared at the screen. Controller Seton's frowning face was turned to one side, and he looked puzzled at some information coming in from another source.

"Sorry, Deputy Director," Commander Seton said, turning back to the screen. "There's been an explosion in the Kenyon mountain city."

"Oh, shit," Jane Oxford said softly from her spot on his office couch. She took a deep drink of scotch and banged the glass down on the coffee table.

Petrie could feel the blood drain from his face. He suddenly felt dizzy. Seton's face went blurry. How could this have happened? All he wanted was either to have Jefferson or the operatives eliminated. He hadn't wanted ten thousand people to die.

He started to cut the connection and slide his chair back when suddenly something happened on Seton's end.

"Wait!" Seton said.

Petrie forced himself to focus on the screen again.

Seton turned away and was staring intently at something out of the vid camera range.

"What do you mean 'wait'?" Petrie shouted at the screen.

At that Oxford jumped to her feet.

Seton simply put his hand up in front of the monitor, showing Petrie his palm.

Quorum Delegate Oxford moved behind Petrie, carefully staying out of vid sight, but in a position where she was able to see his screen.

"Seton!" Petrie said, trying his best to keep his voice low and level, though he knew it didn't sound that level. Right now, the office felt like an oven, and sweat trickled down the side of his face and into his collar. This news would mean the difference between living and being killed in the next few days. And Seton was telling him to wait.

Petrie had no choice. He sat and waited and watched.

Seton frowned and didn't turn back to the screen as he talked. "There's more information coming in from a Bisson satellite that's just passing over that area."

Petrie said nothing

The silence in his office was so intense, he wanted to smash something. Oxford's raspy breathing behind him made her that something. But still he didn't move. He was in enough trouble already, without striking a Quorum delegate.

Finally Seton broke into a smile. "It wasn't a core explosion," he said.

"What do you mean?" Petrie asked, not really understanding. "What kind of explosion was it?"

Seton held up one finger, again telling Petrie to wait, then reached for something off camera. If Petrie had been there, in Seton's command center, he would have strangled the controller by now.

Seton held up a satellite photo of the mountain and positioned it in front of the vid camera, then pointed to a spot on it that Petrie couldn't see that well.

"It looks like a smaller explosion of some sort brought their big landing bay door down," Seton said. "They are exposed, for everyone to see, but there's no sign of radioactivity."

"That's good?" Petrie asked.

"Very good," Seton said, nodding. "It means the backup plan did not happen."

"There was no explosion," Petrie said.

"There was a small one," Seton said. "Something had to bring that big door down. But from what our bio-scans show, there are still close to ten thousand people alive in that mountain."

"Oh, thank God," Petrie said, sitting back.

"The operatives have sent a retrieve signal, as well," Seton said, smiling. "Three of them made it out of the mountain and are going to be picked up shortly."

Petrie just shook his head and took a deep breath. He would be lucky if this night didn't take five years off his life.

He was lucky it hadn't killed him.

"You want even more good news?" Seton asked, now facing the vid screen and smiling like a kid with a secret.

"What?" Petrie said. "I'm not sure I can take much more of this."

"They reported that the target was eliminated," Seton said.

Petrie just shook his head some more. "Send me a full report when you get it," he said, and cut the connection.

"Well," Oxford said, "it seems you and I escaped a very large problem."

"It does seem that way," Petrie said, standing and going to his bar to make himself another drink. If there was ever a time he needed a drink, now was it.

"The question is, what do we do now?" Oxford asked.

"About what?" Petrie asked, stopping halfway through pouring his drink.

"Your little deal with the Shadoon," Oxford said.

Petrie again felt his head swim, and his hand began to shake. He set his glass down and turned to face Oxford. "I'm open to suggestions," he said.

"I assumed you would be," she said, smiling. "I would think that for my silence on this and your special accounts, I should be rewarded. Don't you?"

Petrie didn't like the sound of this, but at the moment he had absolutely no choice but to go along with her.

"I would think so," he said. "What kind of reward were you thinking about?"

She smiled and moved over, and gently kicked a bag tucked in the corner by the shelf. "Seer religious statues might just settle this score."

He sighed and turned back to the bar, then finished pouring himself a very tall drink. Then after one gulp of the cool, biting liquid, he turned to face her. The scotch cleared his mind as it burned going down, sending waves through his body.

"They're yours, and we're even," he said. "There's nine of them left in there."

"I know," she said, smiling at him. "I'll send my aide around for them in the morning."

He nodded as she headed for the door.

At the door she stopped and turned, the smile

that made her a famous and powerful delegate still planted on her face. "I must say, Deputy Director, you sure know how to entertain a woman."

"Always aim to please," he said, giving her his best phony smile.

She laughed. "Oh, I think those statues there will please me just fine." With that she turned and left, pulling the door closed behind her.

It wasn't until the middle of his second drink that he realized the statues had been her goal, right from the start. All the bomb scare had done was just get in her way for an hour or so.

He finished his second drink and started on his third. That hour had reminded him exactly how dangerous this business was, and how close he had come to losing everything. From here on out, he would watch the controllers for these "special" missions much more closely.

And the next thing he needed done was to deal with the unfinished business of the night. Those operatives knew too much.

Tex sat back in the cargo lifter's passenger seat as it left the New Bisson system, heading out into deep space. They had been picked up off the rocks just outside the ventilation tunnel. There had been no Kenyon air resistance or anyone else chasing them from inside. It seemed their stunt of bringing down the big door had caused enough damage to slow them down.

Tex knew it had also exposed the Kenyon to public view. Their secret little city would no longer be so secret.

The flight would take them just under twenty hours, ten times the time they had been inside the mountain.

It had seemed much, much longer.

He had taken off his armor and stowed it with his guns in the one of the passenger compartments that had been given to the three of them. Then he had taken a few sandwiches and a large glass of water and found a chair beside Hawk and Flint in the main cabin area. Both were already eating.

All of them had had their wounds dealt with the moment they had stepped aboard. None were serious. Tex had no doubt he was going to be feeling the aches of this mission for weeks, especially the spot where he had taken the bullet against the armor of his shoulder. He was going to have to work that muscle for some time to get the deep bruise out. He was lucky that was all he would have to do, and he knew it.

When he finished eating, he took the golden statue out of his pocket. It was the one he had taken from Jefferson's office. One of the same statues he had recovered from Dower not more than three weeks before. He studied the alien shape, wondering why the Seers would make a statue representing an insectlike creature that looked nothing like them.

Jefferson's accusations about Deputy Director Petrie certainly rang true now. Especially with this heavy chunk of gold in his hand.

"That's a Seer religious statue," Hawk said. "It's from Jefferson's office, isn't it?"

Tex made sure the pilot's cockpit door was closed, then passed it to her. "It is. It has the bug in it, the one that we traced."

Hawk tipped it up and looked at the bottom, then with a fingernail pried off a small speck. "Amazing how small those things have become."

"What was Jefferson doing with a bugged Seer statue?" Flint asked, taking it from Hawk and studying it.

Tex shrugged. He wasn't certain how much to tell these two. In the world he lived in, information often got a person killed.

"Jefferson was telling us how Deputy Director Petrie had sold us out," Hawk said. "He claimed that Petrie had warned him about this mission. I bet Petrie gave it to Jefferson."

"Warned him?" Flint said, anger in her voice.

Hawk nodded and Tex let her tell Flint everything that had been said in Jefferson's office. Hawk got it right, almost word for word.

"You believe him?" Flint asked when she was finished.

"I don't know what to believe anymore," Hawk said. "That file we found in Blossom could be more than enough for someone to want us killed."

"What file?" Tex asked.

Hawk quickly told Tex about the file they had found in a revolutionary faction's headquarters, and how it proved that the Shadoon had been funding part of the uprising there.

The word *Shadoon* shocked Tex, and it must have shown.

"You know something we don't?" Flint asked, after Hawk had finished.

At that moment he decided to just go ahead and tell them. But first he had to make sure they weren't being bugged. "Hang on," he said, "let me check on something."

He stood and moved back through the small cabin to their equipment storage in the back. There he pulled out a device the size of a pack of cards and held it up for both to see.

Hawk nodded, and Flint actually smiled.

The device would block any bugging equipment with a feedback signal that eventually would blow out the bug itself. The box that Tex held could also tell the operator if any kind of listening device was in operation close by.

He flipped it on, and studied the small read-out panel.

"Nothin'," he said, putting the device down on the floor, still on, and returning to his seat.

"Good thinking there," Hawk said. "I should have done it before I started shooting my mouth off."

Flint just shrugged. "Everything we found we turned in."

"I guess," Hawk said, shaking her head. "I just made too many mistakes this trip. Not sure what's wrong with me."

"You're learning," Flint said, patting her shoulder. "You manage to survive as long as me and Tex here, you won't make those mistakes."

"Yeah," Tex said, "you'll make a whole set of new ones."

"Good to know," Hawk said, smiling. "So what were you about to tell us?"

Tex took a deep breath and settled back sideways in the seat, facing the aisle and the other two operatives. He wanted to be able to see their faces when he told them what he had found on Dower.

"I'm convinced that most of what Jefferson was tellin' us was the truth," Tex said.

"How?" Hawk asked.

Tex pointed at the gold Seer statue on the seat where Flint had placed it. "I found twelve of those on a sand planet called Dower."

"The raiders who were taking out cargo ships?" Flint asked.

"Not anymore," Tex said. "We blew one of their ship's cores, and I barely survived. Two other ops didn't. I found those statues in the basement vault of their headquarters."

"Who did you give them to?" Hawk asked.

"Commander Seton paid me well for them," Tex said, "and said he'd pass them up to the right people."

"Petrie," Flint said, the anger now very clear in her voice.

"I would think so," Tex said. "But that's not all. I found a file there that I destroyed, and told no one about. It named Deputy Director Petrie and the Shadoon."

"The Shadoon, behind a group of raiders who looted cargo ships?" Hawk asked. "Man, those fanatics get around."

"And they seem to be becoming dangerous," Flint said. "Especially if someone like Petrie is being bought off."

"The Dower had a large treasury," Tex said, "and twelve of those statues, so they were fencing the stolen goods somewhere, and getting funds from other places, as well."

"So you think that the statues and part of the money you recovered went directly into Petrie's accounts?" Hawk asked.

"I'm convinced of it," Tex said.

"Which then makes sense of this mission," Hawk said. "We turned in our file, so Petrie knew we had information he couldn't allow to get out."

"And I was the only operative left who knew about the statues," Tex said.

Suddenly to Tex, it did make sense. He and Flint and Hawk were not supposed to have come back from this mission.

"So they send us on a mission we aren't expected to return from." Hawk said out loud exactly what Tex had been thinking. "We take out Jefferson, get killed trying to get out, and Petrie's problems are solved."

"But it seems that by our survivin', we have created an even bigger problem." Tex pointed at the statue again.

"True," Hawk said.

"I would suggest the bigger problem is our knowing he was willing to kill ten thousand people," Flint said. "If that information gets out, Petrie wouldn't last a day."

Tex hadn't even thought of that. He had been so relieved that they had been able to disarm the core explosion, it had not occurred to him how wide the repercussions would be of that core exploding inside that mountain. Even if they weren't Confed, you just didn't destroy an entire city and walk away.

"I wonder who else knows about what almost happened in Kenyon?" Hawk asked.

"I think the answer to that question will determine whether we survive to see another mission or not," Flint said.

Tex could only stare at the golden alien statue and agree. Their lives had become a problem for a number of powerful people, the topmost of which was most likely Deputy Director Petrie.

"So, we take out Petrie," Hawk said.

Tex didn't like that idea. Even though there were more things wrong with the Confederation than he wanted to admit at times, he was still loyal, and that belief was the reason he was willing to lay down his life like he did. Killing a Protectorate Deputy Director, even a crooked one, just didn't sit well with him. It seemed to go against everything he believed in.

"I don't like it," Tex said. "It won't solve any of the problems."

"It will kill the bastard who set us up to die," Hawk said.

Flint nodded.

"How about we deal with him through higher channels?" Tex asked.

"Higher?" Flint asked. "How?"

"It doesn't come any higher than a seated member of the Quorum," Tex said. "I met one of Earth's delegates to the Quorum in a previous mission, and can get in touch with him. He won't take kindly to havin' a dirty Protectorate director."

"You think you can get him to believe you?" Flint asked.

Tex pointed to the gold statue. "I think I have enough evidence to make sure Petrie doesn't help the Shadoon, or any other criminal outfit ever again."

"Do it," Hawk said. "But if your delegate doesn't do anything about him, I'm going to pay a visit to Petrie's office on Wren—a stealth visit—and cut his throat."

"If I can't get the help I need from the delegate, I'll help you plan that mission," Tex said, surprised at the thought.

"And so will I," Flint said.

All three of them sat there, thinking. Tex knew that his very survival over the next few weeks depended on many factors, most of which were out of his control. And he hated having anything out of his control.

Chapter Fourteen

Over time, successful operatives develop a deep distrust for their superiors, and a corresponding reliance on their team members, which can even extend to their clones.

—Commander Nobel,
memo to Protectorate Operations Board

Quorum Delegate Jane Oxford sat in her office chair, listening to the operative code-named Tex as he finished reading a letter of introduction from his planet's Quorum delegate, Frank Lach. Around them, her office soaked up his deep voice without an echo. The oak paneling and leather furniture that she loved made him seem even more out of place.

Tex wore an open dress jacket that looked just a tad too small for his solid frame and slacks that rippled from the muscles in his legs. He clearly was not the type to dress up, and it showed. She had seen pictures of him, but they hadn't done him justice. In pictures he looked to be a normal-size man with a square jaw and short-chopped hair. In person, she realized he was very large and perfectly proportioned.

When she had come around her desk and

225

extended a hand for a handshake, his surprisingly gentle touch had completely engulfed her hand and wrist. She had no doubt that just a normal squeeze from that fist of his would have crushed the bones in her hand without a problem.

She had offered him a chair, but he had asked to stand to read the introduction letter first. She had gone back behind her desk, sat, and listened.

The letter was short and to the point. Simply an introduction.

Considering the events of the last week on New Bisson, she had been stunned when the request for a meeting had come from Tex, through Delegate Lach. She was getting tired of surprises, and it seemed that anything Deputy Director Petrie touched led to a nasty surprise. Now she had a sneaking hunch she was about to get another "Petrie surprise" from this big operative.

Tex kept reading, his massive frame filling her office like no other single person had done before. It was no wonder this man was considered one of the best ops agents in all the Confed. He could scare the enemy with his size alone.

"He has not told me of the exact nature of his problem," Tex read the words of Delegate Lach, "but he has assured me that it is of top priority and pertains to Protectorate Operations security."

Oxford didn't let herself smile. She would bet all her money that Tex had wanted to tell Frank Lach his problem, but Frank hadn't let him. Frank had made it clear to her before, and again now, in the letter, that he wanted no part of any Protectorate issues. That desire to keep his nose clean was one of the things she liked about Delegate Lach.

Tex kept reading. "As the chair of the Protectorate Operations Oversight Committee, I assumed this matter would be best handled by you. I hope you agree."

"I do," she said aloud, nodding to Tex.

The big operative smiled at her, and then reached forward and handed her the letter. "He signed and sealed it," Tex said.

She took a moment to study the letter, letting the silence in the room build. She wished she had turned down the environmental controls a notch, since it was feeling warm, and Tex was clearly sweating. Before the meeting she had pulled the blinds over the window that looked out over the main governmental area, and all the grass and landscaping between the buildings. She figured that for a meeting like this one, Tex would feel more secure with the blinds pulled.

She glanced at Lach's signature and official stamp. She had no doubt at all that the letter was genuine. And since the events in the underground city of Kenyon, she had little doubt what this meeting was going to be about.

She finished studying the letter, for Tex's benefit pretending to make sure it was real; then she laid it faceup on her desk. "Won't you have a seat?" she asked, pointing to a chair to one side of her desk.

This time he did as she asked.

She stood, came around the desk, and sat in a second chair, facing him. She knew that this would give Tex a feeling of confidence, and a feeling that she cared about what he was going to say. Actually, she cared very much, since she had yet to decide what to do about those who knew about the Target Jefferson mission, including Tex and the other operatives.

"I'm not sure where to start," he said, looking almost uncomfortable in the chair.

Even sitting he towered over her. And the shoulders of his jacket looked as if they might rip if he took too deep a breath. She wanted to offer to let him take off his jacket, but she knew that would be wrong for him. This man was very committed to the ideals of the Confed, and she was a Quorum delegate, one of the highest ranking people in the Confed. For him to maintain his respect for everything he fought for, she knew she had to act the part he saw in her.

"Please start at the beginning," she said, smiling. "And take your time. I am sure this is important, because the work you do for the Confed certainly is important."

He smiled and nodded. Then with a deep breath,

he told her about finding the Seer religious statues on Dower.

She did not interrupt, or tell him that the statues were now secure in her safe behind the bookshelf that stood beside her desk. She did not indicate to him in any fashion that she already knew everything he told her.

At least everything until he stopped, hesitated, and then told her about the file he had found and destroyed. The file with Petrie's name in it. With the Shadoon name in it. That news actually surprised her.

"Why did you destroy the file?" she asked after he had finished.

He shrugged, threatening to rip out of his suit again with the movement. "I honestly didn't know what else to do with it," he said. Sweat was running off his forehead. "I was too angry at him to even think clearly at the time."

She could tell that just talking about it made him angry now. And Tex was not someone she wanted to have angry at her.

"Fair enough," she said, nodding. "Is there more?"

"Yes," he said, staring at her. "Have you read the mission report for Target Jefferson in the underground city of Kenyon?"

She smiled. The man was even smarter than he looked. He understood that anyone in her position would get reports from the Protectorate on Operations.

"Yes, I have," she said. "You and the others did a fine job. It is a shame about Earhart, but he will be cloned, from my understanding. He's a good agent, and the Protectorate need agents like him."

"Good," Tex said, looking down at the carpet.

"Is there more you are not telling me?" she asked.

He nodded. "There was a fail-safe on the mission that we did not allow to happen."

"The ship's core explosion," she said. "I know."

Tex's head snapped up, and he looked at her, clearly stunned. There was relief and puzzlement mixed in his eyes. And a touch of doubt now, as well. She knew he had to be wondering if she had authorized such an action in the first place.

"I learned of it after the mission had started," she said, jumping in to clear his obvious worry.

"Oh," he said.

"You can trust that the idiots who came up with that idea will be punished. And the Confed owes you a debt of gratitude for working so hard to stop the explosion and save all those lives."

He nodded slowly. Clearly her level of knowledge had surprised him, and she guessed that he wasn't sure whether to believe her. In his position, she wouldn't.

The silence in the room grew for a moment as

she gave him time to gather his thoughts and go on. None of the activity going on in the huge building could be heard in this room, and she had also made sure that no listening devices would work in here either.

This office was her haven, and she liked the silence it offered, especially at times like this one.

For a good ten seconds she wasn't sure if he was going to add anything else; then the big man clearly decided to go on. With a quick hand movement, he reached into his coat's side pocket, and pulled out a Seer statue.

She stared at it, genuinely amazed. Of all the things she expected him to show her, that was not one of them.

"Did you know about this?" he asked, holding it up for her to see.

"No," she said honestly, trying her best not to let her full surprise show. "Where did you get that?"

"It was given to the target of our last mission by Deputy Director Petrie," Tex said, handing her the statue.

She studied it for a moment, letting the heaviness of the gold statue calm her some. Then she looked up at him. She knew the statue had been given to Jefferson by Petrie. She hadn't expected it to be brought back by the operatives. Or anyone, for that matter. But how this operative knew who gave it to the target was what stunned her.

"How do you know that information?" she asked.

"The target told us," Tex said.

"He *told* you?" she asked, stunned. "Why would he do that?"

"He was trying to buy time for snipers to get into position. And he almost succeeded."

She nodded, staring at the statue in her hands. It was a very ugly thing. But priceless in the larger picture of the developing state of the Confed and the Sword of Shadoon.

"He also said that Petrie was working for the Shadoon," Tex said.

Quorum Delegate Oxford hated surprises, and she was getting far, far too many lately, all caused by the idiot Petrie.

"Really?" she asked, sitting back in her chair.

"I'm afraid so," Tex said, nodding. "And considering the file I found on my previous mission, and the information brought back by Operatives Hawk and Flint on their previous mission, we all felt it was necessary that I bring this to you."

She nodded, letting herself think. Clearly Deputy Director Petrie had overstepped his bounds and was far too stupid to be trusted anymore. Now, even frontline operatives were discovering what a fool he was.

All of this had gone too far. She decided right at that moment to stop it. She needed to wipe the slate clean and move on.

She sat the statue on her desk and stood, indicating that Tex should remain seated. She moved around to a special drawer in her filing cabinet and opened it. Inside she kept a substantial amount of Confed script. In her area of work, there was no telling when cash would come in handy, and this was one of those times.

She took out thirty thousand credits, closed the drawer, and went back to Tex, her arm extended with the bundle. "This is for bringing me the statue and information."

"I can't take that," he said, holding up his hands.

"Yes, you can," she said. "And you will."

Then she smiled at him. "I am aware that operatives make some of their money on what they find on missions, and that you must supply your own weapons and armor at your own expense. You brought nothing but this statue back from the last mission. It's the least I can do."

He hesitated a moment longer, then nodded and took the credits from her hand.

"Trust me," she said, laughing softly. "It is worth far more than that."

Then she leaned against her desk. "And with that in mind, I have one more favor I would like to do for you, to help in some small way repay the Confed's debt to you for saving all those lives."

"It was my job," he said.

"Actually, if you had strictly done your job, you

would have let that ship's core blow up," she said. "True?"

He said nothing, so she went on. "So we are all grateful to you and your team for saving the Confed from a very ugly situation."

"We don't ask for anything in return," Tex said. "It's the nature of our job."

"I know that," she said, putting on her best calming smile, "but it just so happens this job I need done has a very large pot of gold at the end of the rainbow."

"I'm not sure if I understand your meaning," Tex said.

She smiled. "A report of an upcoming and important Operations mission just crossed my desk yesterday. A mission I helped to set up, to be honest with you. It is a raid on an antigovernment base on my home world, Barsaan. This group has been driving my home world government crazy for the past two years, and the group needs to be eliminated before they cause any trouble I can't undo."

"I understand," he said. "And your government hasn't been able to do it?"

She smiled. "Exactly. Also, it just so happens this rebel base has a very large treasury."

Tex nodded, clearly not certain what to think.

"Oh, don't worry, I expect to have my campaign fund see a share of that treasury," she said, laughing, "no matter who goes after the group.

But I would love to use this favor to my home world, and to me, to give me the opportunity to repay you and your team, as well. Will you accept?"

Tex nodded, and smiled at her laugh.

She extended her hand, and he stood. "Expect a call from a new controller named Adams within the next day or so. I am reasonably certain Commander Seton will no longer be in a position of authority very shortly."

Tex nodded as he again gently shook her hand.

"And you have nothing to worry about with Deputy Director Petrie," she said, staring up right into his eyes, his one big hand in both of hers.

She could tell he didn't believe her completely, so she went on. "I can tell you, in all confidentiality, that he has been under investigation for some time now by the Quorum and the Protectorate internal affairs division. With the events of Target Jefferson, he has crossed the line."

"That he did," Tex said.

"In my mind," she said, letting his hand go, "Deputy Director Petrie is clearly a traitor to the Confed and its interests. He will be removed from his office."

"Not just on this, I hope," Tex said, smiling at her.

She laughed again. "No, your information simply added to the already growing list of traitorous deeds."

"Thank you," Tex said, "for telling me that."

"I wouldn't tell you if I didn't feel I could trust you," she said. "And thank *you*, for having the courage to bring this information to me."

He smiled and turned for the door. A moment later he was gone.

The moment the door closed, she moved back to her desk, picked up the Seer statue, and headed toward her safe. She had ten of the twelve now. And she needed to put this away before she got to work cleaning up the mess Deputy Director Petrie had made.

The shelf moved aside easily, and she worked the simple safety features of the safe to open it. A moment later she set the statue beside the others and closed the safe. Then she went to the window and opened the blinds, letting in the light from the beautiful day.

She hated stupidity, and Petrie was just about as stupid as they came. It was going to be a relief not to have to deal with him anymore.

Commander Seton sat at the communications monitor in his office, waiting. A report was due in from the team on Target Duke, and he needed to be on hand to monitor the connection, make sure no one else jumped into the feed.

He had been sitting at the console for more than an hour now, munching a bag of chips, killing time.

Behind him a breeze seemed to blow through the room.

He spun around, his heart racing as he scanned the small area he called an office. It held his main desk, the communications desk he was sitting at, a briefing area, and a couch. All were cluttered with papers and food wrappers.

The door to the hallway was still closed, and nothing seemed to be out of place. There was also no window to allow a breeze in.

"You're going nuts," he said out loud. "Get a hold of yourself."

He took a deep breath to calm his nerves.

The breeze must have been his imagination, or a malfunction in the environmental systems in the building. Nothing more.

He turned back to his screen, shaking his head. Ever since the near miss on the Target Jefferson mission, he had been jumpy, seeing shadows, at times afraid even to move. Director Petrie had been giving him the cold shoulder, as well, not bothering to return his calls, which did not bode well for Seton's future.

Seton had made sure over the last few days that he was as secure as he could get, including spending the last two nights in this command area. Another week, and he would be reasonably sure that the entire thing was past and he could relax. They never let loose ends last that long. But until then, he would remain on guard and would stay very jumpy.

The screen still showed no response from the team, so he did a quick change of screens to check out his accounts, make sure Petrie wasn't trying anything from the money side to get even with him.

Seton had a dozen accounts, all password secured, and on three different planets. He logged into them daily, always in secure ways, to make sure his retirement funds were still growing. Maybe now might be the best time to retire out of this crazy life. If things over the next few days got any more strained, he would do just that.

With a quick keystroke he checked all his accounts, bringing up their totals on screen.

"What!" he shouted, knocking his chair over as he stood, staring at the impossible messages.

Every account had been closed, the money moved.

Gone.

"Petrie, you ass!" Seton shouted, his voice echoing around the empty room.

"I think you may be blaming the wrong person," a voice said behind him.

At that moment an invisible arm wrapped around his shoulder and chest, yanking him back against a hard body, pinning Seton in such a fashion that he couldn't move.

"Petrie isn't smart enough to do something like that."

"How did you get in here?" Seton demanded, struggling to yank himself free.

"It wasn't hard," the voice said behind his head.

Seton struggled even harder, and just as he thought he might make it free from the person's grasp, he felt something yank the skin across his throat.

His first thought was Powerblade.

Only scouts used Powerblades, since they could be used in stealth mode.

His blood sprayed out onto the computer screen that showed his empty bank accounts. The heated liquid streamed down his chest as the invisible arm let him go, shoving him forward.

His mind told him to turn, to lash out, but all his body could do was slam against the desk and slump to the hard floor.

The shimmering of an operative in stealth mode moved the air above him as the world around him went black around the edges.

He tried to call out, but his air only made a hissing sound out of what was left of his throat.

The sound of the control room door opening and closing was the last thing he ever heard.

Deputy Director Petrie paused in the doorway of the restaurant, scanning the thin crowds who were out for leisurely evening strolls. One couple seemed to be in love, looking only at each other. Another man, alone, walked quickly, bent on some unknown destination.

Petrie didn't trust any of them. Everyone was a threat to him now.

Before the Target Jefferson problems, he would have loved joining the walkers. Now just crossing the sidewalk scared him to death.

This was only the second time he had allowed himself to go out in public, and even so his body-guards were around him and well armed. He had even had them check the restaurant kitchen to make sure his food was all right. After that nothing tasted right. And he couldn't relax enough to enjoy even a glass of wine. Why he had bothered to leave his secure home was beyond him.

He flat-out didn't trust Delegate Oxford, and if something came along that made her need him dead, he had no doubt he would have a hard time staying alive, especially out in public.

At the moment he just didn't want to take any more chances. Maybe if he proved hard to kill, she'd just figure he wasn't worth it.

He studied the sidewalk one more time, then the buildings across the street. No one looked suspicious in either direction, no window was open, no one was even looking in his direction.

His guards nodded that he was clear, so he stepped out of the restaurant and headed for the backseat of his limo. The open door was only six steps away, but it felt like a mile.

The night air on Wren smelled wonderful, as always. A combination of roses and raspberry. The temperature was perfect room temperature, and a slight breeze made everything seem fresh.

Evenings such as this one were the reason he lived in Wren. He just wished he could enjoy it. Maybe some evening in the future, he might get the chance to do so again.

Petrie's bodyguards nodded as he entered the car, and then they stepped back.

"Good evening, sir," the driver said, glancing back at him.

Petrie smiled at the driver as the car locks snapped into place, securing him for the moment.

The window between the driver and Petrie's compartment rolled up, and the limo pulled away from the curb. Petrie let out a deep breath and sat back. The limo was bulletproof, and practically bombproof. He was safe for the moment.

He let himself enjoy the sights as the limo sped through the lower section of Wren and toward his home. In another week or so, if nothing had happened, he could start assuming that it was going to be business as usual again. Only with Delegate Oxford in the mix, it would never be completely usual. But he knew he could make both of them some real money, if she let him.

His secure phone beeped beside him, and he

picked it up. The image of Delegate Jane Oxford's face appeared on the screen embedded in the padded wall above the built-in bar.

"I just wanted to bid you farewell," Delegate Oxford said before he could say hello.

She was smiling at him.

"What?"

"Oh, and I wanted to thank you, as well."

"Farewell?" Petrie asked, his stomach clamping as he looked around outside the car. Nothing seemed to be wrong at all. "Thank me for what?"

She laughed, and a chill ran down his spine. Then she took a sip of wine before answering. "The Citizens for Effective Leadership on Barsaan, my home world, is going to be very happy with the anonymous donation of your bank accounts."

"What are you talking about?" he demanded.

Inside his vest he had a Black Pistol a friend had given him years ago. It had been stripped down so that he could conceal it in his jacket. He fumbled for it now, pulled it out, then checked it to make sure it was ready.

She laughed. "That's not going to help you, you know. And neither is your money, since I just had it all transferred."

Her laugh was a nightmare to him, filling the limo like the stuff of bad dreams.

"You can't do that!" he shouted at the screen.

"Oh, actually all the transfers were very simple, and quite impossible to trace," she said, smiling at him. "So don't you go worrying about that now. You have so much more to think about."

"What are you talking about?" he shouted at her.

Then she waved. "Good-bye," she said, smiling.

She was taking a sip of her wine, looking over the lip of her glass at him, when the link was cut.

Suddenly an orange gas started to fill the limo, coming in through the air-conditioning ducts.

"Stop the car!" he shouted through the intercom to the driver.

The car just kept going, only now he noticed that the driver had missed a corner and was no longer heading toward Petrie's home.

"Let me out!" Petrie shouted as the orange gas got thicker, burning at his eyes. He started coughing, which only pulled the gas deeper into his lungs.

He tried to yank open the door, but the locks held. He took a bottle out of the bar and tried to smash it against the window, but the bottle broke, spraying him with a sticky white wine.

The gas blinded him, burned his lungs, made him cough.

He took his Black Pistol and aimed it at the window. The sound of the gun going off inside the limo was deafening. The bullet smashed off the window and into the seat behind the driver.

The window wasn't even scratched.

With his last ounce of strength Petrie turned

around and kicked at the door. It was designed to keep out almost all attacks.

And keep him safe inside.

He wasn't going to get out.

He slumped in the seat, all his energy gone, the pain in his eyes and lungs so bad he could hardly stand it.

The last thought he had as he leaned against the window was to wonder how much Oxford had paid his men to double-cross him.

Chapter Fifteen

Full-body clones can be made to such exacting standards that a wife or husband of the cloned person may not be able to tell the physical difference. Even scars, moles, and persistent rashes can be duplicated. The only limitations are caused by gaps in the memory chips resulting in slight memory loss.

—Dr. Woak,
Medical Chief, Operations Division

Commander Adams had an office like none other Tex had seen. Adams had decorated the place with old-style Earth posters from movies and some strange models of seagoing ships, plus lots of toys. Cars, airplanes, monsters, spaceships. Toys everywhere, filling every shelf space, hanging from the ceiling, stacked in corners and on the back of the couch. Toys of all kinds and shapes and sizes, most of them relating to old movies and vids.

Tex glanced around, at first caught up in the bright colors and strangeness of the room. He had been in a lot of controllers' offices over the years, but never one like this. Clearly Adams was a collector of movie memorabilia, and it seemed as if Tex had just walked right into the middle of his storage space.

"Weird, isn't it?" Hawk said, coming up from behind Tex as he stood in the middle of the room. "Haven't seen anything like this outside of a kids' playground, or a movie museum on Earth."

He glanced back to find not only Hawk, but also Flint. They had come out of a side room with a large table that looked like some sort of briefing area.

"That it is," Tex said, shaking Hawk's hand, then Flint's. "These must have cost him a fortune."

"More like three fortunes," Hawk said, glancing at an old dinosaur. GODZILLA it said on the base. "There's more of it back there and in the bathroom and the hallway."

"I figured you were going to be the next to show," Flint said, ignoring the toy discussion. "After Hawk arrived."

Tex had expected them to both be here, because of the comment made a few days earlier by Delegate Oxford. But he wasn't sure he liked the fact that all three of them were together again so soon after the Target Jefferson mission. It made it just too easy for some "accident" to happen.

"Not happy to see us?" Hawk asked.

"He's worried," Flint said. "It seems logical to get a team together again, especially if that team must be done away with."

"I am worried," Tex said, ignoring her negative comment. "But not much more than usual. I'll explain in a secure place."

He figured they would all have to be extra careful on this mission. And part of being extra careful was waiting to tell them about his meeting with Delegate Oxford until he was sure they were not being recorded.

The meeting with her had been one of the strangest Tex had ever experienced. She had known what he had expected her to know, and been surprised when he had expected her to be. And when he left with the money she had given him for the statue, he still had no real idea whether he should trust her.

If she had been telling the truth, and this mission was to be a reward for their work, that would be fine. But he had decided when the call came, a few hours earlier, that he was going to go into this mission even more alert than he had done on other missions, if that was possible.

But the problem was that on missions he had to trust a number of people, the most important being his team. He trusted Hawk and Flint. He had no reason not to, since they were in the same place he was. But the second most important person who had to be trusted was the controller, and Tex didn't even know him yet.

And there was little doubt that whoever this controller was, he would be working in some fashion for Delegate Oxford. There was just nothing about this situation that made Tex feel comfortable.

"Our host," Flint said, nodding to the door toward the room with the table.

A moment later Commander Adams came in. Tex was shocked. He couldn't be more than thirty, if that, and had one of those faces that looked even younger. He seemed perfectly at home in the midst of all the posters and toys that surrounded them.

He was tall, with long arms and legs, and a smile that filled his face with an innocence of youth. He moved like he knew how to move and take care of himself. Tex had no doubt, just from first glance, that the kid was very fast, and very tough.

"Tex," Adams said, sticking out his hand. "Glad to have you on board this one."

Tex shook Adams' strong hand, nodding, but saying nothing. Clearly Flint and Hawk had already met him.

"I'm surprised you re-formed this team," Flint said to Adams as Tex let go of the man's firm handshake.

Adams laughed. "Are you kidding? After word got around about how you saved that last mission, I pulled strings to get you three on this one."

Tex wanted to say that more than likely it was Oxford who pulled Adams' strings, but instead he said nothing. Letting Adams keep up his little show of control hurt no one.

At that moment the door to Adams' office complex opened, and another man walked in, carrying the traditional bags of an operative. He did the same thing Tex had done: got three steps inside and stopped and looked around at the strange and colorful decorations.

"Jacks," Adams said, moving over and shaking the new man's hand. "Come and meet your other team members."

Adams did a quick introduction.

Jacks had dark eyes, dark skin, and a hard face with a scar across the top of his brow. He was as tall as Adams and almost as tall as Tex, and moved with the same assured motions. Clearly Jacks had been on a number of missions before, and meeting new team members was nothing new.

Tex did notice something odd, however. Jacks smiled at Hawk, nodded to Flint, and stared at Tex as the introductions were being made.

All three reactions indicated to Tex that Jacks had known who they were before he stepped through that door. Since Tex had no idea who Jacks was, that bothered him.

"Okay," Adams said, clapping his hands and heading through the door into what was a briefing room. "Now that everyone is here, let's get started."

The initial briefing around the big table stayed pretty much along the lines Oxford had laid out in her office. The group threatening Oxford's home world government had been growing stronger and stronger with each passing month. And with each month they had become more daring, more directly challenging to the government. There had been threats to overthrow the planetary government, a member of the Confed.

"They are called the Wendigo," Adams said.

"Wendigo?" Hawk asked. "Where does that name come from?"

Adams shrugged, shuffling some papers in front of him. "Not a clue, actually. Some call them Dwellers in the Cold, but on this planet the name Wendigo is feared, respected, and hated, depending on who you're talking to."

"Why?" Tex asked. This was a detail Oxford hadn't mentioned.

"Barsaan is in the midst of an ice age," Adams said. He flicked a switch on the edge of the table and brought up a holographic image of their target's planet. The image floated over the center of the table, turning slowly.

It was clear to Tex that Adams was right on the money about the ice age. Over a third of the planet's surface was covered by ice and snow. And from what Tex could tell, the cities were all clustered at the equator.

"So the colonists went to the equator," Hawk said. "Are the Wendigo colonists there, as well?"

"No," Adams said. "They live on the ice shelves and maintain major camps in both polar regions."

"Why?" both Tex and Jacks asked at the same time.

Adams shrugged. "Who knows why colonists set up where they do. They've been on those ice shelves for more than a hundred years now."

"I didn't bring enough clothes for this mission," Hawk said, shaking her head at the sight of their target.

Tex had to admit, he wasn't liking this much at all either. He had hated the heat of desert planets, but never had he been dropped into an arctic region before.

Adams laughed. "Don't worry, I'm supplying special cold suits built to withstand temperatures far lower than it will get."

"Weapons?" Tex asked. He doubted his machine guns would work in extreme cold conditions.

"Supplying those, as well," Adams said. "And trust me, it's worth my investment. We'll all be rich if this works out."

No one said a word for a moment; then finally Jacks asked, "So what or who is our target? And how do we get all this money you're talking about?"

Adams nodded, flipped a switch, and the holographic image of the world disappeared over the table, replaced with the image of a man dressed in white fur of some sort. He slowly turned so that all four of them could see him from all sides.

"Sincar," Adams said, pointing at the man, "head of the Wendigo. We take him out, and scatter the rest of them into the cold, and they won't be a problem to this planet's government for years, if ever."

"And the money?" Jacks asked.

The image of the world came back, with a red dot glowing on one of the white areas near the northern pole. "This is where Sincar lives and runs the Wendigo. There's a very large treasury located in that base."

Tex just stared at the image of the red dot on the white ice. He didn't like how this mission was shaping up at all.

Three days later, after working out exactly how they were going to get into that ice-covered base, he liked it even less. There were just too many things that could go wrong, and over the years he had learned that when that was the case, something always happened.

And rarely was it good.

Jane Oxford sat at her desk and let herself sip a glass of wine as she watched Commander Adams' face appear on her screen. Around her the office building was silent. She had a hunch that, since it was well past midnight, she was the only delegate left in the building. She was going to regret the late night when she had to attend the morning Quorum session, but there was no way she could go home with this one last detail left to take care of. One last loose end from the Target Jefferson problem.

"The mission is under way," Adams said. "They just touched down."

"How long?"

"Less than twelve minutes from touchdown to end," he said.

"I want to be informed the moment the mission is over, and the outcome is certain."

Adams laughed. "The outcome is not in doubt. These are the Wendigo. They have been paid well."

"We can only hope you are right," she said, and cut the connection.

She sat back, forcing herself to take a deep breath and sip the one glass of wine she was going to allow herself tonight. She hated cleaning up other people's problems. And this mission would be the last cleanup of Deputy Director Petrie's mess.

Unless, of course, it somehow created another mess of its own.

She glanced at her watch. Twelve minutes was a very long time. She might have to have a second glass of wine.

Around her the silence of the building weighed heavy, and for the first time since she had taken the office, she wished she had ordered a music system installed.

"Thirty seconds to touchdown," the pilot announced.

"Everyone ready?" Hawk asked, glancing around the interior of the cargo ship. For some reason Adams had not managed to get them a nice corporate shuttle this time, but instead they had been forced to endure the last ten hours in transit on a cargo ship that had been stripped bare of everything but four seats anchored against the ribs and wall plating.

The flight had been bumpy and noisy and cold, and Hawk had been glad when they entered orbit and started to get ready.

Everyone wore the pure white environmental suits over their armor. The suits would supposedly protect them from the cold and make them almost impossible to see on the ice sheet. Even their weapons were white.

All of them had taken extra care not to allow even a single stain on the white suits while transporting and putting them on. Out in the pure white of the snow, where their target was, a single black grease smudge from the cargo ship would show up like a flashing sign.

"Ready," Tex said, nodding as he snapped his

goggles down into place, basically hiding his face. He had a special laser cannon in his hands and another over his shoulder.

"Bring it on," Jacks said. His goggles were already in place and his weapon over his shoulder.

"Ready," Flint repeated.

Hawk braced herself against the edge of the cargo plane fuselage, her feet wide, both hands holding on to the exposed structure of the ship. She was being careful not to rub against anything that might leave a mark on her suit while at the same time making sure she did not take a tumble if the ship landed hard.

The landing jarred them, made the ship creak, but nothing more. She had ridden through a lot worse.

"Down," the pilot reported over the comm link.

Hawk slapped the button that opened the hatch, snapped her goggles up into place, and made sure her rifle was ready to fire. As always, she was going to be the first out.

Her heart was pounding, just as it always did, and her stomach was twisted in a knot. No matter how many of these missions she went out on, her heart pounded every time. She had no doubt that wouldn't change in the future.

The hatch slid out with a clang and then down, forming a ramp to the snow below. The intense cold hit her in the face like she had been slapped, swirling white flakes into the ship.

"Wow!" Jacks said behind her. "That's cold!"

He was right. Even through the protective gloves and goggles, the cold bit, and bit hard.

In three running steps she was down the ramp and out onto the ice.

The wind was blowing hard from the direction of the nose of the ship, and by the time she had reached the bottom of the ramp, she couldn't see a thing. Complete whiteout.

She moved left, making sure of every step, using the display in her goggles to tell here where she was going. There were no other bio-signs visible on her built-in screen, which so far was a good thing. Their biggest planning fear was to land right in the middle of a bunch of guards. It seemed that hadn't happened.

The ship was supposed to have landed in a shallow valley, but from what she could tell on her radar display, she was on a smooth plane without cover. If there ever had been rocks here, they were long buried under the blowing snow and ice.

She did a quick calculation. The target's home was ahead, right where it was supposed to be. At least they got that much on the money.

"Going right," Flint said.

Hawk's heads-up display inside her goggles showed a green blip moving away from her to the right. Another green blip moved straight ahead away from the ship, followed shortly by a fourth.

Jacks third, Tex last, as planned.

They had prepared for snowstorm conditions, but nothing like this. She held up her rifle in front of her. It was nothing more than a faded shape through the blowing snow. Regular sight wasn't going to help them.

"Clear of the ship," Tex said.

"I'll be waiting for your call," the pilot said.

On her radar display, Hawk saw the ship lift off and vanish. Even though she wasn't more than twenty paces from it, she didn't actually hear it or see it.

All she could hear was the intense blowing wind.

All she could see beyond her goggles was white.

With a snap she flipped on her infrared, switching her mask over, as well. Everything in front of her took on a pinkish color, and the snow became less of a barrier. Now the rifle in her hands was clearly outlined. With infrared she could almost see ten steps. Not much of a visual range, but better than it had been.

"How far to the target?" Tex asked.

"Six hundred paces," Hawk said.

"This is gonna be impossible," Tex said.

"Everyone switch to infrared and sonic," she said.

"Copy!" Tex said. "Better."

"Copy!" Flint said.

"Already there," Jacks said.

"Then let's move out," Hawk said. "Spread formation."

Being careful to not lose her footing, she stepped forward, paying almost as much attention to the images on her display as the infrared sight through her goggles. She trusted the bio-signs and the radar more than her own sight in these conditions.

Around her the cold whipped at her suit, her hands, her face. The wind was a constant roar in her ears.

She had no doubt that any skin that might get exposed would soon have frostbite. Adams had warned them the conditions would be rough, but not this rough.

Why would anyone in their right mind colonize this kind of place? There was just no accounting for taste.

Suddenly, as if the very snow in front of her had taken on a life of its own, a form rose up. Whatever it was, it had been lying prone on the ground, blocked somehow from her bio-readings.

The form had a rifle aimed at her.

She almost had time to bring her rifle around when the shot hit her squarely in the chest. The sound was muffled, and vanished in the wind like a ghost.

The impact smashed her over backwards.

She landed squarely on her back, her rifle long gone from her hands. Or at least she couldn't feel it anymore.

In fact, she couldn't feel anything anymore.

Her mind told her to jump back up, attack, or at least shout out and warn the others, but nothing in her body worked.

She had no doubt she had been shot.

Think! she ordered herself.

The shot had caught her solidly in the chest, more than likely smashing her spine.

She had no idea why it didn't hurt. Shouldn't a wound like that hurt?

She tried to move her legs, but couldn't even feel them.

A form crouched above her, pure white against the blowing snow, nothing more than a shape outlined by the wind.

She tried to reach for it, but her arms wouldn't move.

Nothing would move.

Had she been drugged?

The pinkish-white of the snow in the infrared swirled around, making her dizzy.

The form over her still didn't register as a bio-form on the display in her goggles. Maybe it was a ghost?

No! Ghosts didn't shoot people.

A warm feeling crept up through her chest,

flowed along her back. In the cold it felt wonderful.

She knew she shouldn't be feeling that way,
thinking that way, but at the moment it just didn't
seem to matter anymore. She just hoped someone found her after the mission, and got her chip.
She had enough money in her accounts to pay for
the cloning.

The outline of the white figure patted her
shoulder, like a father patting a child.

She wasn't a child. More than anything she
wanted to reach up and take off the person's goggles so she could see his face.

She should be able to see the face of the person
who killed her.

Or hear the voice.

It would be nice to see something more than an
outline and hear something more than the wind
before dying.

But she knew that wasn't going to happen.

The form stayed over her, watching her, as the
world faded slowly from infrared. She closed her
eyes, letting the darkness come.

And then even the sound of the wind was gone.

Tex could not believe the cold.

Nothing in his worst nightmares had prepared
him for this. By the time he had taken twenty
steps, even with the special suit and gloves over
his armor, he could barely feel his fingers. And he

had no doubt his toes would be frozen long before they made it to the target's home.

If this was Delegate Oxford's idea of a reward, he was going to have to have a word or two with her. From the looks of this, they were walking right into a trap, and a trap that was going to be almost impossible to fight their way out of.

On the display in his goggles all he could see ahead was nothing but smooth, snow-covered ice. With the help of infrared, he could barely make out the back of Jacks, who walked just ahead, and to Tex's right.

This wasn't good. Not good at all.

Hawk's and Flint's long-range abilities were worthless, and without cover, they were simply walking targets. This was about as bad as it got.

"Hawk!" Flint said. "Respond."

Tex stopped, noting on his display that Hawk had stopped five steps back.

Nothing.

"Malfunction?" Jacks asked.

Tex felt his stomach cramp up. On his bio-display, Hawk's sign flickered, and then vanished. Either it was a malfunction, or Hawk was dead.

She was too far away for him to see her, or to have even heard a shot if someone had fired.

"Group up!" Tex ordered into his comm link.

Flint started toward him, but Jacks stepped to the right and vanished into the snow.

Suddenly Jacks' bio-sign vanished, this time without even a flicker.

Tex held his laser cannon ready, slowly turning in a circle. There was no cover, no place to retreat to. If Jacks and Hawk had been killed by an enemy attack, he and Flint were going to have to fight it out right here in the open. Or make a dash for the target's underground headquarters and run right into more of the enemy there. But fighting in corridors was a lot better than fighting out in the open, when the enemy couldn't be seen.

Flint appeared out of the blowing snow to his left just as the ground around them seemed to move. It was as if the snow itself was growing, becoming alive.

Five figures, all lying prone on the ice, raised rifles and fired at him and Flint, almost at the same moment. It was as if he had walked to the exact spot he was supposed to walk to, allowing them to get the best shot.

At this distance, he wasn't even going to offer them decent target practice.

A shot slammed into Tex's left arm and spun him around just as he returned fire with his laser cannon.

His own shot went high and wide.

It seemed so strange. The wind and suits kept all the sound out, so the shots were either silent or very muffled. And through the infrared, everything had a pink tint to it, as if already coated in blood.

He staggered, and then regained his balance. He wasn't going down yet.

Beside him, Tex could tell that Flint had been hit, as well.

She staggered backwards, as if getting away from the attack, and he moved with her. His left arm was useless, and blood was flowing from his suit and freezing on his chest from a second wound he hadn't realized he had received.

He could feel the pain in his arm, but he ignored it. All he needed was one arm to fire a laser cannon.

Two other silent shots smashed into Flint, spinning her like a rag doll. He wanted to reach over and catch her, but he didn't. Instead he fired back at the white forms on the ground. He couldn't tell if he hit them or not.

On his display, Flint's bio-sign went dark.

She was gone.

But she kept moving, her machine components keeping her body active and fighting. He had heard that the old synthetics could keep going even after their bio-parts were dead. Something about the last thoughts of the human acted like orders to the machine parts.

Flint raised her gun to fire into the storm, but another shot cut through her neck, snapping her head half off.

Her body fell to the snow. She twitched a few times and lay still. Now even the machine in her was dead. Whoever was firing must have known exactly what it took to stop a synthetic. And they had done just that.

This entire mission had been a phony. Nothing more than a trap to get rid of him and Flint and Hawk.

If he got out of this alive, he would kill Delegate Oxford.

His finger pressed down on the laser cannon, firing into the blinding snow as two more shots smashed into him. His armor deflected one, but the other got through, burying itself in his gut.

They were using projectile weapons of some sort, with armor piercing rounds.

He went to one knee, offering them a smaller target as he kept firing. If he was going to die out here, he was going to take as many of the bastards with him as he could.

He fired blind into the wind and snow, moved a degree to his right, fired into the storm again, moved a degree, fired into the storm again. He just wished he could use both guns, but his one arm had been shattered.

He caught a glimpse of one form moving through the blowing snow to his left.

He turned and caught the man with a laser shot, smashing the shadowy white form end-over-end through the storm.

From his right a shot ripped into his already bad shoulder and arm, sending waves of intense pain through him. That made him even angrier.

He spun, firing, over and over, not letting up.

The person who had shot him paid with his life for the action as Tex's laser beam cut the figure in half.

From behind Tex another unexpected shot caught him squarely below the neck.

Tex's armor didn't have a hope of stopping it.

He slammed forward into the snow, twisting just enough to land and roll facing upward. His mind wanted his arm to bring up the laser cannon and keep firing, but now it seemed nothing worked.

A moment later, a form appeared above him.

He willed himself to reach for it. Strangle it. Kill it.

He couldn't move.

Four people were holding him down, one on each arm and leg. The man standing on his smashed arm would die for the pain he was causing, if Tex ever got up from the ground.

"Nice job," Jacks' voice said. He was standing over Tex, his laser rifle aimed at him.

Tex could see the outline of the op, but his bio-sign didn't appear on the display in front of his eyes.

Neither did the others who stood around him, holding him down, all protected in white suits and goggles. The bio-scan displays must have been rigged, as well.

"Kill them," Tex said, blood in his mouth making his words sound odd even to his own ears.

Jacks laughed. "I can see now why she wants you three cloned. You got six of my friends here before they got you. She's not going to be happy with that extra cost."

"Kill them," Tex said again, not wanting to believe that another op had been part of the trap.

"Sorry," Jacks said. "I can't and don't want to do that. I'm just here for some chips. Sort of a glorified delivery boy for our good friend Delegate Oxford."

Jacks leaned down over Tex, the snow covering his face and head, making him look like one of the monster toys in Adams' office.

With all his will, Tex tried to make his body move, lash out at Jacks, but nothing would. The men on his legs struggled and held him, the two on his good arm held it pinned, as well.

"Quit struggling," Jacks said as he positioned what looked like an ice pick above Tex's chest right over his heart. "You'll be back soon enough, good as new."

The next moment the pain of the blade in his heart shot through his body.

Tex jerked upward, yanking one of the men

holding his good arm, jerking him across his chest.

"Man, you're one strong mule," Jacks said.

Those were the last words Tex heard.

Epilogue

The silence in Delegate Jane Oxford's office seemed more intense than normal as she read the final report on the Target Sincar mission. The mission had been on her home world, and three top operatives were lost. While she read, she had pulled the blinds over her window and given her secretary instructions that she was not to be disturbed, for any reason. She needed to concentrate fully on this last task, just to make sure nothing had been missed.

To the members of the Protectorate board and her oversight committee, the mission had been a standard affair that had gone tragically wrong. As she read the report in her hand, all the details backed up that scenario.

The transport had landed in a highly guarded area, and in terrible weather conditions. The operatives, facing trained fighters who were used to the conditions, hadn't stood a chance almost from the first step.

The report went on to state that if it hadn't been for the quick thinking of operative Jacks, all three of the other agents would have been lost to the Confed forever. Jacks had called for emergency retrieval, and under heavy fire, had managed to get back on the cargo ship with the three dead operatives' chips in his possession.

The report finished with the amount of bonus credits Jacks was rewarded for his heroic actions.

She dropped the file on her desk next to another report and sat back staring at the document. She and Jacks were now the only two left in the Confed who knew the entire truth of what had really happened on the Target Sincar mission. Commander Adams had met a very untimely death at the hands of a small time crook just a week ago. Very unfortunate.

Operative Jacks was the only loose string she was going to allow, and she had left him loose for a reason. She wanted him alive, just for his value to her in future projects. It was worth the risk, considering that even if he did decide to do the insane thing and speak out against her, who would believe him? She had enough information against him to have him executed as a traitor to the Confed. She held all the cards.

She glanced through the report one more time, then nodded, now sure that she had missed nothing. Then she picked up the second report. She read it slowly, making sure of every detail.

The second report laid out the plan for the successful full-body cloning of the three operatives killed in the Target Sincar mission. The extra parts needed to repair Flint's neck and back had been found in a stockpile of synthetic tech left over from the Machine Wars.

Four top Operations Division memory-chip technicians, all of whom were qualified to do this sort of work in Confed Region Six, were enlisted to wade through the data contained in each team member's chip. The technicians had carefully erased the short- and medium-term conscious-memory code from the chips, leaving everything else that was tagged as long-term memory, including skills and tactical memory.

No reason was given for the erasures, no report was ever written. However, the scientists had known that such removal of all short-term memory had been a theoretical possibility since the early days of full-body cloning. It was thought to be very difficult, and was strictly forbidden.

The implantation of the chips into the clones had occurred without problems.

The report ended by stating that all three agents would need counseling and help in their recovery. All three would be given different cover stories to explain their need for medical attention and loss of memory. None would be told they had been cloned, as was standard procedure.

She dropped the second report on top of the first, leaned back, and sighed. The entire mess that Deputy Director Petrie had caused was now cleaned up. The Confed had kept three top operatives, but lost two crooked controllers and one crooked deputy director.

Good.

She stood and pulled open the blinds, allowing the sun to again fill her office. The day was beautiful in more ways than one.

She let the rays warm her skin for a moment, then moved over to the bar hidden under a countertop. With such a successful outcome, she figured she deserved at least a small toast.

She poured herself a snifter of brandy, then took a sip, silently toasting the operatives and the ten golden statues sitting in her safe.

It was good to not waste resources. No matter what the resources were.

Tex put his weapons bag down beside a chair and looked around the controller's headquarters. It was sparsely decorated, with only a briefing table, five chairs, a computer console, and a small reception area where he now stood. Even the couch and two chairs were basic, no-frills types. All the colors were grays and browns.

The walls were even bare, and painted an off white.

He shook his head. Controllers were a strange bunch, that was for sure. Each of them decorated differently. Judging by the lack of decorations, Commander Bratton was going to be a no-nonsense type.

Tex could live with that. Having a controller who was all business could be better for the operatives under his control. Details didn't get missed, little things that might mean the difference between life and death.

He paced, letting some of the energy he was feeling take form. He was eager to get going. It had been some time since his last mission, and until the last month he hadn't realized he had missed the action. Now, this close to a new assignment, he wanted to get going, get back into the game. He was tired of facing doctors and pumping weights.

For a while there the Operations Division doctors in charge of his recovery weren't sure they were even going to allow him to go on another mission. But finally, with hard work, he had proved to them he had recovered from his fall, that he was fit and ready to help the Confed again.

Behind Tex the door into the main hallway opened, and a man entered. He was tall, a bit on the heavy side, with a wide forehead and receding hairline. A faint scar ran from his widow's peak to just above his right eyebrow. He had the look of a controller who had seen combat, which was reassuring.

"I'm Commander Bratton," the other man said, extending his hand. "Glad to have you on board this mission, Tex. Your reputation precedes you."

Tex nodded, and clasped the hand. "Glad to be on my feet again."

Bratton looked at him closely. "Heard you had a nasty fall."

"Must have been," Tex said, laughing, "since I don't remember much of it."

Bratton chuckled easily with him, and right at that moment Tex decided he could be trusted.

"I know you've had some experience with aliens before. Ever hear of the Ferals?"

Tex shook his head.

"Nor has anyone else. They're a race native to a planet in the Ulysses system. They're a little rough around the edges, but would be useful allies of the Confed if they decided to join, and right now they could use our help. I'm in charge of providing it."

Bratton pointed a thin file folder at him. "You're all I've got to work with at the moment, but I'm hoping to get a scout on board, goes by the name of Hawk. She's young, but already building a reputation."

Tex had a fleeting sensation that the name

seemed familiar, but dismissed it. Didn't ring any bells. "I can work with just about anyone."

"Good." Bratton turned and headed toward the briefing table half covered with maps and status reports. "Well, let's get to work."

The excitement in Tex's stomach rose as he turned to follow. It was great to be back.

YOU'VE READ THE BOOK.
NOW LIVE IT.

www.BruteForceGame.com

And don't miss this official tie-in to
the thrilling Xbox™ game: *Crimson Skies*

CRIMSON SKIES™

based on the Xbox game Crimson Skies™:
High Road to Revenge

by Eric Nylund, Michael B. Lee,
Nancy Berman, and Eric S. Trautmann

Welcome to the world of *Crimson Skies*.
The United States is a land torn apart by
epidemic and war. With chaos on the
ground, America's highways have been
forced into the skies, a lawless new frontier
where the flying ace—hero, pirate, villain—is
king. Here are the exciting, danger-packed
adventures of three such daredevils.

Published by Del Rey Books.
Available wherever books are sold.

Check out the official prequel
to the award-winning Xbox™ game: *Halo*

HALO™
The Fall of Reach
by Eric Nylund

**As the bloody Human-Covenant War rages on
Halo, the fate of humankind may rest with one
warrior, the lone SPARTAN survivor of another
legendary battle . . . the desperate, take-no-
prisoners struggle that led humanity to Halo—
the fall of the planet Reach. Now, brought to
life for the first time, here is the full story of
that glorious, doomed conflict.**

*This novel is based on a
Mature rated video game.*

**Published by Del Rey Books.
Available wherever books are sold.**

**And look for the thrilling new Halo novel,
coming this spring 2003!**